Praise for Katharine Duckett's
Miranda in Milan

"What happened to *The Tempest*'s Miranda when she left the island and returned to Milan with Prospero? Duckett's *Miranda in Milan* has the answer: love and lust, mothers and monsters, magicians and masked balls—all delivered with queer Shakespearean Italian Gothic panache."

—Nicola Griffith

"Glorious and transformative, this may not be the continuation Shakespeare intended, but it is the one that we deserve."

—Seanan McGuire

"*Miranda in Milan* is a wondrous tale that turns Shakespeare's world sideways, to reveal everything he left out—and to show us that the greatest magic comes from claiming your freedom."

—Charlie Jane Anders

"*Miranda in Milan* is somehow both utterly charming and

perfectly sinister, and altogether delightful. A pleasure for any lover of romance, myth, and magic—whether or not they're fans of the Bard."

—**Cherie Priest**

"Katharine Duckett has made Miranda the heroine she always should have been. This beautifully written fantasy is full of court intrigue and family secrets, marking Duckett as a writer you're going to read for years to come."

—**Daryl Gregory**

"This book is for everybody who ever wondered if the wizard Prospero maybe wasn't that great of a dad. Delightful!"

—**Elizabeth Bear**

"Gorgeous and engrossing, *Miranda in Milan* gives us a look at what happens when a fish out of water returns to her pond, forever changed."

—**Mur Lafferty**

"Unsettling, romantic, and intricate, Duckett's debut builds a house of horrors within the walls of Shakespeare's rich, strange work."

—**Max Gladstone**

"Duckett's novella expands the world of Shakespeare's tale in wonderful ways. Part Gothic, part romance, part mystery, and perhaps most of all a novella about working one's way out of the assumptions of a sheltered life, *Miranda in Milan* is a delight."

—**Malka Older**

"*Miranda in Milan* is a marvel of a story, full of strange and powerful magic, love, and other wonders. A brilliant take on what happens after the close of *The Tempest*."

—**Kat Howard**

"With gorgeous prose and an unflinching understanding of the characters she's been given, Duckett has crafted a deeply satisfying finish to the story Shakespeare started telling."

—**Sarah Gailey**

MIRANDA IN MILAN

KATHARINE DUCKETT

A TOM DOHERTY ASSOCIATES BOOK

NEW YORK

MIRANDA IN MILAN

Copyright © 2019 by Katharine Duckett

Cover art and design by David Wardle

Edited by Carl Engle-Laird

A Tor.com Book
Published by Tom Doherty Associates
175 Fifth Avenue
New York, NY 10010

www.tor.com

Tor® is a registered trademark of
Macmillan Publishing Group, LLC.

ISBN 978-1-250-30631-9 (ebook)
ISBN 978-1-250-30632-6 (trade paperback)

First Edition: March 2019

For Laura.
Shall we stick by each other as long as we live?

Graves at my command
  Have waked their sleepers, oped, and let 'em
    forth
  by my so potent art.

—Prospero, *The Tempest,* V.i. 53–55

O, wonder!
How many goodly creatures are there here!
How beauteous mankind is! O brave new
    world,
That has such people in't.

—Miranda, *The Tempest,* V.i. 203–206

Miranda in Milan

Chapter 1

When Miranda came to Milan, she found she was a monster.

She'd been given a queen's welcome in Naples, that lovely city on the sea, but as they'd moved inland, the warm breeze had left them, and she found herself among stony-eyed strangers who refused her gaze, who seemed loath to touch her flesh. They treated her like Caliban, her ladies-in-waiting and royal relatives.

They arrived in Milan on a cold, gray day, and as they approached, the castle of her ancestors looked more like a prison than her rightful home. Its high ramparts stretched into the mist, leached of color by the pendulous clouds, and its black mouth gaped wide, swallowing them as their carriage passed through the gates. Miranda trembled, for she could no longer see the sky. Her whole life through, sea and sky had surrounded her: with neither in sight to give her bearings, she hardly knew where she was.

Her father had vanished into the labyrinth of the castle as soon as they arrived, seizing back the rooms his usurping brother, Antonio, had taken over while Prospero was in exile, gathering his left-behind books, and sequestering himself in his libraries to pore over the new tomes that he demanded his servants bring him right away, the advances in alchemy that he had missed while on the island. He left her with barely a word after ordering the servants to settle Miranda into her rooms, though he had insisted that she accompany him here, to see her home once more before she married Ferdinand and settled in Naples.

"I thought we *were* married?" she'd said, in the carriage. He had turned to her, eyes still on the countryside out the window, and replied, "Hm? Oh, yes—but marriages of princes are contentious things, and the island where you were wed exists on no map. We'll let the Neapolitans take care of the formalities, the law. There's no hurry, now that we've returned."

She did not understand what this meant: she knew nothing of law, or of marriage, or of the nuances of love, though she did her best to grasp their meanings. Her father had never spoken to her of these matters in any depth, and now, in her rightful homeland, she began to realize how much she did not know, how much she could not ask. The island they had left behind held fathomless mysteries, but it also moved to natural rhythms Miranda could observe and decipher: the animal cries that rose and fell with dawn and dusk, the changing patterns of certain leaves that signified shifts in the seasons. But she could not work out the chaotic patterns of the men and women of the mainland, and she especially could not fathom why they recoiled from her, why the ladies at her elbows hurried her so from place to place, why they made her wear a full black veil, its lacy darkness obscuring her vision like storm clouds moving over sun.

Only a few weeks before, she had felt jubilant on the shores of her island. For a dozen years she and Prospero had lived in isolation on their lonely stretch of sand, cast out from their homeland after her uncle Antonio usurped her father and claimed the dukedom of Milan for his own, and for Naples. Prospero told her the sad tale of how Antonio had worked with the king of Naples to bring about Prospero's downfall, using scurrilous claims about his magic to unseat Prospero from the throne and turn good men against him. Her father had shipwrecked Antonio and the Neapolitans on their humble isle in order to bring his perfidy to light, revealing her uncle's evil deeds.

"Now," her father had proclaimed to the assembled men, his clever plan complete, "we will fly swift to Italy, and my Miranda will claim her birthright as a duke's daughter and take her place beside noble Ferdinand as princess of Naples."

She'd watched Ferdinand embrace his father, King Alonso, with tears of joy, for each had thought the other drowned in the storm that brought them to this strange isle, the storm her father had created. Her father had his arms around Gonzalo, the counselor from Naples who had shown them kindness many years before, giving them provisions that had seen them through their terrible journey at sea. Rightful order was restored, their sorrow was now ended, and all was well in Milan and Naples once more.

Yet her uncle Antonio's silence disquieted her. He stood outside the circle of warmth, speaking not a word as the air around him rang with laughter and glad cries. His chilly hush, she thought at first, must of course owe its cause to the exposure of his treachery. But no, she saw shock upon his face, as though he had glimpsed some ghast there, on the beach, some vision that chilled him to the bone, even in the island's gentle heat.

Yet it was not Prospero he looked upon with haunted, salt-burned eyes.

It was her.

~

The only person in Milan who did not treat Miranda like an abomination was Dorothea.

They sent Dorothea into Miranda's room on her seventh day in the castle. No one had said a civil word to her in a week: the servants always scurried in, moved around her as though she were a cockroach, and locked the door on their way out, their faces far paler than when they'd entered. They would let her leave her quarters if she asked but insisted on having a girl dress her, to force the hated veil over her face. And so she had chosen confinement. At least here she could remain herself, barefaced, unobserved. The two opulent adjoining rooms with their painted walls and gilded trinkets became her cave, and she had begun to feel like a badger, fierce and frustrated and afraid of the strange two-legged creatures all around her.

She had begun to poke at those who entered her den, asking them, again and again, why she could not roam the castle freely without the cumbersome veil over her face, the veil that felt as though she had run face-first into a clump of spiderwebs. She demanded to see her father but was told that he was cloistered in his quarters, or in important meetings with emissaries from far-flung locales that he could not possibly interrupt, or simply unavailable every time she asked. Beyond their curt responses to her queries, none of the servants spoke more than a dozen words to her: that is, until Dorothea.

Miranda had sulked at the girl at first, unhappy at the

presence of yet another individual who would try to bind her into a corset or tame her curly hair, all the while managing to gape, recoil, and block her exit in concert. She'd never asked for servants: she'd never wanted them. She could manage perfectly well on her own.

(Well, that wasn't entirely true: she had wished for an Ariel of her own, once. An ethereal slave to do her bidding, like those under her father's command. But when Prospero found her cultivating one of the small island spirits, he beat her black and blue. Since that day, Miranda had learned to handle her own affairs.)

"So they sent you to gawk at me, did they?" She sat cross-legged on the bed, in the pose that had infuriated the maids who'd unpacked her things. "The savage? The feral girl? What tales do they tell of me in this dank, dirty castle?"

The girl continued to dust and tidy, never slacking. "It's a beautiful castle, my lady. If you ever left your room, you'd know."

Miranda leapt from the bed, snarling. "You had better not take that tone with me. I'll—I'll—"

"You'll what?" The girl was only inches from her now, amusement plain beneath her placid expression. Miranda racked her brain. None of her usual threats to Caliban applied, or vice versa. She couldn't shove the girl into the sea, or drop her from a cliff onto the eastern rocks, or command Ariel to scrape out her innards and feed them to the gulls.

She folded her arms. "I'll tell my father."

"Your father," said the girl, turning back to her cleaning, "does not hold as much sway here as you think he does."

"Why are you talking to me this way?"

"Because I'm a witch. I have nothing to fear from you or your father."

"A witch?" Miranda examined the girl, whose black hair and hazel eyes looked plain enough. "Like Sycorax." She stepped back, dark memories flooding into her mind. "Then your magic is no match for my father's."

"Your father's magic relies on books." The girl knelt to attend to the floorboards. "And everyone says he threw his books into the sea."

For this Miranda had no retort. This girl, she saw, did not flinch beneath her gaze or avoid her eyes. "Do the others know you're a witch? All the others living in this castle?"

"They know." Dorothea rose, setting her hands on her hips. "It's why they sent me to deal with you. They're as afraid of me as they are of you, but they think perhaps I can tame the monster."

Miranda grimaced, baring her teeth: an old habit, one learned from Caliban, who used it to intimidate her. She corrected herself, pursing her lips, waiting for the girl's mockery; but Dorothea didn't laugh. "I don't think you're a monster, though. I hope you know that. I think you're alone, and scared, and that you come from very far away. You don't know the customs here, and that isn't your fault. My family didn't either, when we first came to these shores. But we learned. You can learn, if you want to, in time."

"I do not wish to acquire the customs of people who behave so barbarically," Miranda retorted. That was her father's language: the only language, other than Caliban's, that she had ever known. But her voice lacked conviction. She had wondered, these past days, what she did want from her homeland. What she wanted from the people who treated her like an unsightly specter, and what she desired to hear when she asked, over and over, if there had been any word from Naples. As badly as she wished to leave Milan, Miranda hardly knew anymore if she wanted to be with Ferdinand. He had not turned out to be the man she imagined when she encountered him in that golden grove on the island. No sooner had they returned to Italy's shores than she saw him begin to cast his gaze about, admiring every beautiful woman they passed. Miranda knew those mooning looks; they were selfsame as those she had treasured when first they met.

Thinking of it now, watching Dorothea dance her way

around her room as she attended to the chores, she could hardly blame him, for these creatures, these women of Italy, moved like sea waves and laughed like the chimes of her isle's evenings. She yearned for their kind glances, though they never had any to spare her. They shouted and scintillated, and oh, she thought she had discovered marvels when first she looked upon the faces of new men. But women: women were another wonder entirely.

"I've found that barbarism varies from land to land." Dorothea began to shake out the curtains, and Miranda came out of her reverie, realizing she'd been watching the other girl's every movement the way she once watched swallows flitting through the trees back in her island home. "I've lived in cities all over, from sunny Marrakech, where I was born, to Córdoba to Cologne to Constantinople. Neighbors often called neighbors barbaric, even though they looked and acted and ate almost exactly the same way."

Her words gave Miranda pause. Civilization, her father had always stressed, was what separated Miranda and himself from savages like Caliban. Civilization guided them in their decisions, while Caliban behaved like an animal, with no moral compass or history to draw upon. Prospero and Miranda sprang from a mighty and cultured civilization, and though no hint of that civilization lay around them, he'd explained, they were still elevated by it, still responsible for creating it wherever they traveled. Miranda, who had never witnessed more than three mortal people gathered together until King Alonso's ships came to her island's shores, didn't firmly grasp the concept. Long ago she had thought of civilization as a thin, shimmering cloak, something like the aura she could see around Ariel. She saw no glow on her own skin, though, and felt no noble lineage leading her through life, no matter how often her father promised her that birthright.

"Constantinople." Miranda sat down on the edge of the bed, considering the word. It sounded funny and not at all like the names of other places she knew. "These other cities you lived in—are they in Italy too?"

Dorothea turned her way, her tan skin perspiring lightly from her labors. "They're not. They're far away. Maybe farther than your island. I only came to Italy four years ago, when my mother died, and Milan two years after that. Picked out a new name, learned the language, and that was that. My sister and brother came here with me, but they're gone now."

"They're dead too?"

To her astonishment, Dorothea laughed. "They really didn't teach you any manners on that island, did they?" Miranda flinched, and Dorothea waved a hand. "No, no, I'm not laughing at you. Really. I'm laughing because if you'd said that to anyone else, they would have turned red as a beetroot, and now I wish you had." She came closer to where Miranda sat. "It's not considered polite to go around asking people if their loved ones are dead, you know. At least not without knowing them a little better."

"I . . . You're right. It's just that I've never known anyone whose brother and sister died before. I've never known anyone *with* a brother and sister before."

Dorothea perched on the edge of the bed, crossing her ankles. She raised an eyebrow at Miranda, as though daring her to say something, but Miranda held her tongue. Why shouldn't Dorothea sit on her bed? It was too big for Miranda anyway. She missed her cozy nest of blankets and pillows in their little house on the island, where she would snuggle up by the fire when the wind blew cold and sleep without coverings in the summer. "They didn't die. My sister met a man, and my brother did, too. She followed her husband to the New World, and he's in Orléans with his French soldier."

It hadn't occurred to Miranda that men could wind up with men, but she supposed it made as much sense as a man ending up with a woman. Her knowledge of these affairs, as her courtship with Ferdinand had shown, was woefully scant. "What's in the New World? What's so new about it?"

Dorothea grinned. "It's new because we just started

sending ships there, I suppose. And it's different and wild. Mariam couldn't wait to go. The man she married is an explorer." She got up from the bed, gathering up the rags and dusters she'd used on the room. "Speaking of exploring, I should tell you before I go that there's more than one way out of these rooms."

"If you mean the window, I don't know how I'm supposed to climb in these dresses."

"Not the windows—the tunnels. If the common people rise up against you and your cruel and excessive reign, you have to get out one way or another, don't you? So the old dukes built escape tunnels that lead from the royal rooms into the passages beneath the city, or so the other servants say. I'd bet you all the gold in this castle that there's an entrance to one here."

"Where?"

Dorothea shrugged. "How would I know? I'm a common person." She started for the door. "And I have to be getting back. Those noble closestools don't empty themselves, you know." She paused, her hand on the doorknob. "Unless there's something else you need?"

Miranda cleared her throat. "I—" *Want you to stay*. The girl was nothing like Caliban, but something about the way she spoke reminded Miranda of the only friend she had ever known, though they were friends no longer. "I . . . could use an attendant. One assigned to my care.

There's lots—there are many things that are new to me, here. I'd . . . I'd like your help."

Dorothea arched an eyebrow, a smile playing on her lips. "To learn our barbaric customs, you mean?"

Miranda smiled back, surprised at the relief she felt. "Yes. As I suppose I have to learn them . . ." She cleared her throat, suddenly shy. "I'd like it to be from you."

Dorothea gave an exaggerated bow, a clear mockery of servitude. She moved with big, expansive gestures, and there was something about her face Miranda liked to watch, the way her eyes crinkled up at their edges; the way her lips pursed as she prepared to smile. "As you wish, my lady. I'll see if they'll allow the witch and the monster to fraternize on a more permanent basis." She turned to leave, then turned back, stepping forward to take one of Miranda's hands. Miranda froze as Dorothea raised Miranda's hand to her own lips, pressing a small kiss into the skin. "And in the meantime—don't despair. I'll come back soon, one way or another."

She stepped through the doorway, leaving Miranda once again alone. A chill passed through the room, and Miranda shivered, feeling that there was someone standing behind her: but when she turned to see, there was no one there.

∾

She waited a long while after Dorothea left to begin searching the rooms, afraid that the girl would return with a guard to catch her in the act. That was the kind of thing Ariel would do: goad her into action with a few well-placed words and then arrange for Prospero to discover her in some minor transgression. She'd learned his tricks long ago, but she didn't know if mortals played different games. So far in this life she had encountered not a single soul who proved to be what they seemed upon first meeting.

A different girl, not Dorothea, brought in Miranda's supper without speaking and then whisked it away again, returning briefly to light a fire and prepare Miranda for bed with as much haste and as little contact as she could manage. Miranda waited until she heard the girl's footsteps recede far down the stone hall and then threw off her covers, rolling off the bed to look beneath. No trapdoor lay in wait.

She stood, casting her gaze about the room. Heavy tapestries hung from every illustrated wall; jutting stones, from floor to ceiling, looked as though any one might be a secret lever.

Miranda reached out and ran her hands along the perimeter of the room, feeling for cracks and catches as she moved from the first room of her chambers to the second. It was difficult to make out any anomalies by the light of the fire, and her fingers scrabbled fruitlessly over the stone, finding no purchase.

Frustrated, she turned her eyes upward, examining the high vaulted ceilings. They were decorated on every side with scenes of golden-haired beings, winged creatures that reminded her of Ariel. Her gaze wandered from their skies and fell upon the far wall, which was covered all over in paradisal scenes of animals and trees. Upon it hung a weaving that depicted a serpent and an eagle, facing off.

The room had grown drafty, and the tapestry fluttered slightly, though the others around it hung straight and still. Just above her head, in the center of the serpent's green belly, Miranda thought she could make out a bulge. Or was it only a shadow?

She took a chair from the table by the window where she ate her meals—until her manners improved, she had been told, she would not be permitted to dine in public—maneuvering it as well and quietly as she could to line it up with the bottom of the tapestry. Then she climbed, pulling the edge of the hanging back from the wall.

There, underneath the basilisk, was a painted pond of rippling cerulean, with a silver fish in its center. The fish was raised a few inches from the wall, and from a distance of even a few feet away it would seem to be part of it, but

Miranda could see now that it was a handle. She grasped its scales and pulled, and the pond peeled away from the wall, revealing a round portal into darkness.

She glanced behind her, though she knew she was alone. Her nightgown was hardly made for climbing, but Prospero hadn't allowed her to keep any of her clothes from the island better suited to this purpose. "You're a child no longer, Miranda," he had told her. "You're a lady of Milan, and you will present yourself to your people as such."

"And yet they hide me under a veil," she grumbled, running her hands along the opening's edge. "So what does it matter?"

She could not see how long the tunnel was or what lay within. Spiders, toads, and rats and mice didn't scare her: she'd explored the island's caves many times and grown used to the feel of small legs skittering over her skin. Her true fear was of the space itself, of being trapped in this passage, which wasn't much bigger than her body. Anyone could come into her room, at any time. This place was not her own. And if she was discovered, what then?

She thought how Caliban would mock her as she wavered. "Coward!" he'd say, as he did when they were young. "But then all the members of your sex are fearful little lambs compared to a man like me. *I'm* not afraid."

"*You're* not a man," she'd retort, and then she'd give

in, jump from the cliff or tumble down the hill or swing from the hanging rope across the ravine. And Caliban would follow close behind, chagrined, but never truly angry, never far from Miranda's side: at least not until that day Prospero found them sleeping together, as they sometimes did after a long day at play, and began to rave, beating Caliban so badly he had refused to so much as look at Miranda for a year.

Her father had cowed Caliban, but her father was not here. Her father could not see into Miranda's rooms. And so she hoisted herself up, slipping into the narrow entrance. She moved forward on her hands and knees, into the blackness, the firelight fading behind her.

The tunnel sloped, gently giving way to a larger, lower passage. Now she could stand, and she saw that the tunnel branched, and that someone had lit torches farther down the way. She crept along the wall, careful of her steps, quiet as she could be in her slippered feet.

She followed a curving offshoot of the main passage and found it led to another portal, this one on a low, angled wall just above her head. She prodded, and it gave way. She pushed again, an inch at a time, until she could peep through the gap, to see where in the castle the tiny door let out.

She was looking up at a man's ankles and feet. Huge, heavy feet beneath long robes. She recognized those stone legs, and the back of the head, crested with laurels, that she could see rising above them. She was in the long hall on the level below her own rooms that led to the ducal courtyard, at the base of the statue of the ancient man who towered there, whose name she did not know.

Suddenly she heard voices coming down the passage and ducked back into the tunnels, breathing hard.

If she were caught, perhaps her father would beat her, but she had been beaten before. He always spared her the worst of his fury, and in the end he would be happy to see her, she was certain. He had told her once that her face was proof of miracles untold, that her very name reflected its wonder. She had been proud of that, before coming to Milan, where it seemed every citizen shunned her countenance.

Miranda walked on, choosing her path by the light, never taking the brightest route, but always keeping some illumination in her sights. Her sense of direction was sharp from years on an island where rocks sometimes got up and moved, where trees occasionally began to complain and shift themselves from place to place. She'd had to make a map in her head to navigate the isle freely.

Here the tunnel was nearly as wide as a road, arched and set with smooth bricks on all sides. She walked along it for a time, until a movement within one of the dark apertures caught her eye. She thought, for a moment, that she saw a spark of aurulent light dance across its shadows, the kind of magic spark she had seen fly from her father's fingertips, and again her heart began to pound. But peering into the cramped passage, she could see it was unlit and seemed utterly deserted.

She glanced about and took up a torch from the wall of the covered road, making her way down the dark shaft.

The passage curved, and Miranda followed it, losing the light behind her. She could only see a few feet in front of her until the tunnel debouched into a larger passage, this one with small, high windows on one side that let in a little moonlight, bathing the stones below in a bluish glow. On the side opposite, she could see a large iron door. It was open.

She passed through, casting her torchlight ahead of her, and found three smaller rooms encircling the entrance, each with its door hanging open, almost as if someone had just departed. They fanned out from the spot where she stood, and she saw the rooms were part of a half circle, a self-contained space whose purpose she could not immediately divine.

She could make out low long tables in the room to her right, and here and there the floor glittered with what looked like the dusty remnants of crushed glass. It reminded her of her father's laboratorium back on the island, which he rarely let her enter. Once he'd brought her in to show her a new toy he'd made her, a little frog that hopped when he brought a finger to its back. It croaked, too, but not the croak she had heard from real frogs on the island: more of a creak, like it hurt its mouth to move it. "Alchemy," her father proclaimed, "is a divine art, with aims that reach far beyond the mortal realm. We seek to deliver the gifts of the gods into the hands of man, to bring gold down from the heavens, to grant life unending. Why should our stay upon this earth be so precious, so brief? The spark of life, Miranda, can be summoned where no life lay before. The spark of life is ours to create."

She hadn't understood his words, but she had taken the small creature in her hands, where it sat trembling. When she examined it later, alone, she saw the stitches in its side, in the skin that felt almost like a real frog's, though harder and colder. She saw that its eyes were made from black pebbles, pushed into its face. She released it outside, and when it would not jump without her prodding, she took it to a far pond and sat it on the muddy bank. She hoped it might find a home there, but the other frogs leapt away from the creature as soon as she set it down. For many months, she did not return to the pond, but when she finally did, the little toy frog was gone.

She began to step farther into the warren but stopped

when she heard a sound. Close. Far too close. The sound of breathing, heavy and low.

Her legs tensed. The sound seemed to come from one of the unexplored rooms to her left.

She stayed still, listening, but the sound did not move closer. She should turn back. She should flee at once, as fast as her feet could take her. But curiosity pulled her forward, as it had propelled her so many times as she traveled along her island's shores. Never, despite her father's warnings, despite the insect bites and the scratches and the gashes, had Miranda ever been able to resist an adventure.

The room was empty. A wooden table stood against one wall: otherwise the space bore no trace of human presence. Yet she could hear the breathing still, sounding now as though it came from the walls themselves. She had the dizzying sensation of standing within a living lung, feeling the blast and crush of breath all around her.

She spun slowly, throwing light onto each wall by turn. As it passed over the curve of the wall opposite the door, she saw a slender rectangular crevice set into the stone. She approached, as silently as she was able, and pressed her face against the gap.

She looked into a cell hidden behind the wall of rooms. There, crumpled in a corner, was a man. A man she knew, a man whose face mirrored her father's. Her uncle Antonio.

He was asleep, his black hair splayed out on the stone floor, his gaunt torso twisted, for his hands were cuffed by long chains to the wall. She had missed what had become of him in the excitement of their arrival in Milan: nor, she reflected, had she seen much of him during their few days in Naples. He had worn the same dazed expression every time she'd glimpsed him since that day on the island, but he had walked free during their travels across Italy. Her father claimed to have forgiven him. Why, then, was he shackled in this secret enclosure?

Within the cell a chain rattled, and Antonio lifted his head. She could not see whether he had opened his eyes, even as he began to speak.

"And so the storm comes to our shores." His voice seemed crusted with rust, as though he had not spoken for days. "And so Milan is lost, even though I had sworn to save it, even as I thought I had secured its reaches for all the generations yet to come." A glint, in the darkness: yes, her uncle's eyes were open, and his gaze had fallen upon her face. "What must you never do, when dealing with the Devil, girl? Turn your back to him, and give him time. Time, and books, and the sanguineous sea."

Miranda turned on her heel and fled, speeding back the way she had come, the web of tunnels passing in a blur. She barely breathed until she scrambled back through the portal in her wall, nearly toppling over the chair, and dove for the cover of her bed, her breath coming at last in dry, heaving gasps. What was the meaning of his strange speech, his muttered nonsense? Would he tell her father that he had seen her? She knew Prospero's anger would be terrible if he found she'd had any contact with the traitor, even if she told him she hadn't meant to.

Her breathing calmed as she lay in bed. No one came to her door. She closed her eyes and tried to understand what she had seen. She resolved not to tell Dorothea about any of it yet, about the tunnels, about Antonio, even though she yearned to share what she had discovered, to ask Dorothea what she knew. She knew from experience how adept her father was at drawing out information, how he extracted it from Caliban with whips and lashes, and from Miranda's own lips with tools more subtle. If Dorothea had been sent to spy on her, maybe her father wanted her to find Antonio. Maybe this was some kind of test. Dorothea seemed anything but duplicitous, but Miranda couldn't risk a secret like this.

They could speak of other things. They could spend time together, here in her room, as long as she held her tongue, as long as she told Dorothea nothing that might provoke her father's wrath. As long as Miranda was careful, perhaps they could be friends.

Chapter 2

Dorothea returned to Miranda's quarters two days later.

She came with wine, smuggled in under her skirts, though she had been sent into Miranda's room on the pretense of taking Miranda's measurements for a ball gown.

"What is it?" Miranda had asked as Dorothea poured the substance, red as blood, into the glasses she'd brought.

"You'll like it," Dorothea had promised, an impish grin on her lips. And Miranda had: it reminded her of the drink her father made from berries on the island, though this stuff was much stronger.

They sat together at the table by the window, watching the weak winter sun cut across the barren trees. "Doesn't the sun ever shine here?" Miranda despaired, watching the last of the rays disappear. "I don't think I remember what sunlight feels like." She was only allowed to leave the castle on Sundays, when she was taken, without Prospero, to attend Mass in the vast, unfinished Duomo di Milano, which she'd heard her fellow churchgoers joke had been under construction since the Ascension. Heavy fog wreathed the cathedral most mornings, its Gothic spires sticking through the clouds like swords. Once inside, Miranda liked the sight no better: the man with thorns in his hands on the wooden cross made her think of Ariel, knotted and bound in the bowels of a tree. Caliban's mother, Sycorax, had entrapped Ariel in the rift of a cloven pine long ago, until Prospero came to the island and freed him, turning the spirit's powers to his own purpose.

"Milan is awfully drab in the winter, it's true," Dorothea said. "It's lovely in the spring. Much more colorful. You may be happier here then." She leaned forward. "What is it like where you come from? Is there a winter there too?"

Miranda found herself unable to answer in her surprise. Ferdinand and the rest had entertained the court in Naples with tales of her island, exhibiting Miranda, with her quirks and gaps in knowledge, as the prop for their stories of their adventures abroad. But no one had asked her in any detail about her world, before now.

She told Dorothea how she used to measure the seasons, of the tiny purple-green frogs that laid eggs in the pond in the first weeks of spring, of the fragile pink blossoms that began to appear in the low bushes near her cottage. Stories spilled from her lips as she recalled the wonders of the magical island where she had grown into adolescence, of its marvelous music and temperate breezes and bounty of wild fruits.

Miranda trailed off, ashamed of speaking at such length, of disclosing the details of the strange life that had made her a pariah in her native land, and Dorothea sighed. "It sounds wonderful. Really wonderful, like the places you read about in books." She tilted her glass, letting the last of the drops within run down her throat, and Miranda turned her head away. Her face felt hot, and though she now wore much less than she did outside of her rooms—a simple dress, without all the layers and frills of her more formal garments—her clothes weighed heavy on her too. Back on her isle, she had worn the lightest garments she could, to run faster, to jump higher, to escape the heat and feel the sea wind on her skin.

"You had a brother, didn't you?"

"I—" Miranda turned back to Dorothea, startled. "A brother? Do you mean Caliban?"

"Caliban." Dorothea rolled the name around on her tongue. "I knew it was something like that! Most of the girls won't say his name, you know. They think it's some kind of curse."

You taught me language, and my profit on't is, I know how to curse. She shook Caliban's words from her head, her flush spreading from her cheeks down to her chest as she remembered how they had spoken to each other, in her last days on the island. "He wasn't ... my brother." She drew a breath. "He was there before we came. Is that what people say? That he's of my blood?"

"That's the rumor—one among many. They say your father bedded a witch, and she bore him a son. That they were both driven out to sea, but your father killed the witch and tried to raise the wild boy alone."

Miranda shook her head. "No. It's not—why would they say that of my father? Isn't he their duke? Aren't they happy to have him returned, and the usurper gone?"

Dorothea watched her for a long moment. "So he's a good man, your father."

Miranda opened her mouth, but her jaw hung slack. "He's ..." From what she learned of God in her weekly Masses, he seemed something like her father: master of great forces, though not always heedful of their effects. He was kind to her, most of the time. He was brilliant, and eloquent, and when she was young she believed the sun rose and set on him. Yet she remembered the way her father had tortured Caliban: racking him with cramps; taunting him with demons; chasing him and caning him, beating him about the head until his face grew puffy and red, leaving him to cry in the dirt. And she had other visions, hazier, of far more heinous acts: of her father pulling Sycorax's bones from the shallow grave in which they lay, making them dance before Caliban as he wept in the firelight, the blackened skull grinning, the rotted teeth clacking. She thought these only nightmares, in the morning: but hadn't she felt the heat of the fire, the thorny branches brushing her calves? Hadn't her father caught sight of her, and then—

And then—

So many of her memories ended this way. Strange sights, inexplicable visions: and then sleep, a heavy, sudden sleep she never experienced here, on the mainland. Sleep, if anything, eluded her now: she lay awake in her father's drafty castle, listening to all its shudders and echoes, longing for the intoxicating music of her lost isle.

She felt Dorothea's hand on hers and fought the urge to pull away. "I don't ask to upset you." Dorothea insinuated her way into Miranda's line of sight, ducking down to catch her eye, to bring a hand to Miranda's chin and tilt it upward. "I don't know your father, or his history. I don't hold the grudges the old families of Milan do. But . . . there was a reason your father was sent away, wasn't there? Haven't you ever wondered what it was?"

"Trickery. Treachery." Antonio had coveted the dukedom and forced her father out. There was no mystery there. Only the deception of kin.

"Yes, but how? What did your uncle tell them, to make them send their duke away? Hmm? Even if he gave them a pack of lies—don't you wonder what those lies were, and why they rang with truth?"

Miranda felt herself slipping, like she was standing on crumbling soil at a cliff's edge. "The rumors." Her throat was dry. "What else do they say, about my father? About me?"

Dorothea hesitated. Miranda tightened her grip on the other girl's hand. "Dorothea. Please. Tell me. What do they say I am?"

"A ghost."

"A ghost? What do you mean, a ghost?"

"I don't know what it means." Miranda started to protest, but Dorothea stopped her. "I swear to you, I don't. The other girls don't talk to me much. I'm a witch from foreign lands, remember? But I overhear things. I heard them talk about Caliban. And about you. And they called you—they said you were—"

"A ghost." She swallowed. Her father was capable of unimaginable feats: Had he crafted himself a daughter? A filial spirit, docile and deferential? Was that the crime Milan had banished him for? Her free hand ran along her thigh, finding reassurance that she was there, that this body held firm.

"They're afraid to talk too much about your father. They never say his name. And the older ones, the ones who remember when you left, they never talk about him at all. They slap the girls if they hear them gossiping. But when they first brought you to the castle, I kept hearing one word, whispered when they thought no one could hear. In the streets, in the servants' quarters: everywhere I went. Over and over: *Bice. Bice.*"

"Bice." Miranda tried out the unfamiliar word on her tongue. "But what does it mean? Is it a name?"

"You mean you don't know?"

Miranda growled, snatching back her hand. "Of course I don't know! I don't know anything about your stupid city, these terrible lands. I don't want to know what lies they tell about me in this hellish place. I only want—" Her breath caught in her throat as tears welled in her eyes. "I only want to go home."

"I didn't mean . . ." Dorothea watched her with wide eyes. "I'm sorry. I wasn't calling you a fool. It's only . . . I thought you knew. *Bice* . . . it's an eke-name. For your mother's name, Beatrice."

"My . . . mother?"

"You don't remember her?"

"No." Her early memories of Milan were locked away in some shadowed corner of her mind, lost to time, save for a few random glimmers. And her mother—she never thought of her mother. She knew, of course, she must have had one, but she had always been incurious about the woman who gave her birth, the woman who must have died before they departed Italy's shores. "Why . . . why haven't I thought of her? I never asked my father about her, Dorothea. Doesn't that seem strange? Why would I forget my mother?"

"Maybe he wanted you to."

They sat in silence a long time, those words ringing in Miranda's head. Her father, who could reshape the world to his whims, would not hesitate to reshape her mind. She could hear that truth as Dorothea spoke it. She felt she was stepping outside of herself, seeing the world in a way she never had before. It terrified her. If her mind was not her own—her body, maybe someone else's too—

"Miranda." Dorothea's voice, soft as a lute, slid through her panic. "Look at me, Miranda."

She did. She saw Dorothea's open face, her brown-green eyes, the color of a vernal pond as sunlight played over its surface. She anchored herself in those eyes and calmed her heaving breath. "Good." The other girl placed both of her hands on Miranda's wrists. "Breathe deep. I don't know what your father has done, but it's in the past. You're here. You're alive." She pressed the spot where Miranda's heartbeat pulsed. "I can feel it. You're no ghost, Miranda. Though if you stay locked up in this room, you may become one."

Miranda let out a hoarse laugh, something like a sob. Dorothea smiled. "Let's leave here, eh? Go for a walk.

Only down the corridor: only so that you can see past these walls. It will make you feel better, I think." She stood, extending a hand. "Come on. Let me dress you."

Miranda obeyed. Obedience, so far in life, had been her only virtue. And she longed to trust Dorothea, though some part of her still urged caution. Some part of her—the future wife of Ferdinand, the proud daughter of Prospero—compelled her to send Dorothea away, to tell her keepers of the girl's calumny, of the seeds of doubt she had sown in Miranda's mind. But though they had not known each other long, it pained Miranda to think of the betrayal she would see on Dorothea's guileless face. As they stood this close, with Dorothea wrapping the brocaded silk around her waist, slipping her fingers down Miranda's spine as she fastened and smoothed, Miranda could not fathom banishing her.

Dorothea, at last, placed the veil over Miranda's face, and then they walked into the cool of the castle's halls, where torches flickered to light their way. "Have you seen the portraits?" Dorothea asked, threading her arm through Miranda's. Miranda shook her head. "Let's go and see them. I'm sure there were no painters on your isle."

Dorothea pulled her along, telling Miranda of a room they should see, one painted by a famous artist to look like a garden, flowering indoors. Miranda followed in a trance, trying to make sense of her surroundings. This was meant to be her castle, she knew. Meant to be her home. But every time she walked its floors, she felt as though she were walking into a new world, frigid and alien, one she would never understand.

They came to the portrait gallery, which stretched into the darkness of the encroaching night. Old men and women stared out at Miranda from the walls: men and women who looked like her father, with his aquiline nose, his leonine features. She thought of what Caliban would say about these staid, unhappy figures, what epithets he would hurl as he slandered their ostentatious garb, their snobbish expressions.

Dorothea was looking at her, bemused: Miranda didn't realize she'd been laughing out loud. "What is it?"

She released Dorothea's arm, moving closer to the portraits. "Oh, it's nothing. Only . . . I thought of what Caliban might say. He wouldn't understand this at all. These people, their faces: he would hate them on sight."

Dorothea laughed too. "They do look pompous, don't they? This one"—she moved towards the painting of a balding man with the countenance and bearing of a toad—"looks like he must have terrible piles." Miranda burst into giggles, scandalized. "What? I know an ointment that could help him. Very effective."

They walked the length of the hall, and Miranda got as

close as she could to the lifelike images, luxuriating in the ability to examine each small wrinkle and curve of the painted faces, to stare as she could not with living people. At the hall's end, she came to a portrait of her father with a beard brown rather than gray, his hand resting on a silver-tipped cane, his hawkish eyes monitoring the empty corridor in which she stood. It did not startle her, for Miranda was used to her father appearing at unexpected moments, surfacing at one end of the island when she had thought him at the other, catching her in the midst of conversation with Caliban or the island spirits. What caught her attention was the portrait beside his, of which she could only see the corner of a thick golden frame: the picture was draped with a shroud, its material not unlike her own black veil.

She glanced at Dorothea. "Do you know why they keep this one covered?"

Dorothea shook her head. "It's always been that way. I've never looked beneath."

Distant footsteps echoed down the hall. Miranda moved towards the portrait as if mesmerized, taking hold of the cloth. Why had they covered it? She lifted it one inch, and then another. There was a shoulder, in a scarlet garment, and then a collarbone. The curve of a jaw. Rose-colored lips. And then—

"You, girls! What do you think you're doing?" Miranda dropped the cloth and turned to see a woman she recognized, though the woman had never deigned to introduce herself, a woman who looked a little like her and might be a cousin or an aunt. "Get away from there." She strode across the gallery and seized Miranda by the wrist, pulling her back towards her rooms. Miranda caught Dorothea's eye, but Dorothea looked even more frightened than her.

Miranda was dragged through the halls back to her chambers and thrust inside. She heard the locks tumble into place: and then, silence. She fell upon her bed and wept.

Towards midnight, as she counted the chimes of the church bells, she heard a scratching at the door. She ran to press her face against it, to peer into the crack at its base. "Dorothea?" she whispered, placing her fingers beneath. She felt the pressure of a hand on her own, an almost phantom touch, cold and fleeting as the castle's drafts: then it vanished, without reply, and she heard no more until morning.

Chapter 3

She received no word from Ferdinand or his royal father as the days stretched on into weeks. She'd given up asking if there were any letters, any missive that meant her exit from Milan was near. Her heart still leapt whenever she heard a knock upon her door, but the servants brought her only the same heavy, doughy meals, the same bland pastas and meaty stews. She missed the fruits and leafy greens of the isle, and she was unused to eating animal flesh. Caliban killed rabbits on the island, sometimes, and her father had taught her how to catch fish to roast over the fire, but she seldom used the skill. As she pulled the creatures from their safe waters they twisted in torment, their fragile bodies shivering in the sun. The memory of their anguish flavored her palate, draining all pleasure from the taste.

Dorothea did not return for five days, and when she did she bore a bruise on her cheek, an ugly green splotch, which Miranda ran her fingers over, aghast, when the other girl came into the room. "It's nothing.

I would heal it faster, but then they'd whisper black magic, and I'd be in more trouble than I am."

Miranda embraced her, whispering in her ear. "I'm sorry. I didn't think. I should have known they'd hurt you more than me."

Dorothea pulled back, wiping her eyes. "Stop all that. I'm used to a little trouble, eh? But that woman—*Agata*." She said her name like she was spitting. "She's a menace. Treats the servants like animals. Treats animals even worse, probably. Antonio never liked her, but your father has given her run of the place."

Miranda thought of imperious Ariel, who made her blood run cold. "I'm not surprised. My father has rarely valued kindness in his deputies." She beckoned towards the table by the window. "But come, sit. We haven't seen each other in so long! Can't you stay awhile and talk?"

"They still don't trust me." Dorothea began to move about the room, pushing things into place. "I'm only here because two of the other girls fell ill, and they needed someone to clean."

Something in her tone aroused Miranda's suspicion. "'Fell ill'? Your potions or ointments wouldn't have anything to do with that, would they?"

Dorothea smirked, turning her attention to Miranda's wardrobe. "Some small stomach pains, nothing more." She winked at Miranda. "They'll be fine! And if they're not, I have the antidote cooked up already." She began to dust and scrub, and she and Miranda talked for a time of nothing, of anything but their troubles, relishing each other's presence. What a thing it would be, Miranda thought, to see each other freely. To speak as they liked, whenever they pleased.

Dorothea concluded her chores and took Miranda's hand before saying goodbye. "Your father is putting on a ball in two days' time, and you're to attend. To show all of Milan how beautiful the duke's daughter is, even if they still hide her face beneath a mask. They'll let me come back then." She grinned. "And I may have a surprise for you."

"A surprise? What do you mean?"

Dorothea placed a finger to her lips, shushing her. "No more questions. I only hope someone taught you to dance on that island of yours."

"Dance?" She'd seen the spirits dance, but she had not joined in with their revels for years. "I'm expected to dance?"

Dorothea laughed. "Yes, dance, and twirl, and do all that the finest young Milanese ladies do." She gave Miranda a kiss, this time on the cheek. "Don't worry. It won't be so bad. Everyone will be drunk within the first hour, anyway. They'll hardly pay attention to you."

She departed with a farewell, and it was only minutes after that Miranda realized that she'd forgotten to ask about that night, about Dorothea coming to her door, and about that fleeting touch, the one that now seemed like a distant dream.

~

Dorothea and two other girls came to her rooms to wrap her in layers of finery on the afternoon of the masquerade. Agata followed, and Miranda seethed as she stalked around the room, giving orders, examining every inch of Miranda's form. The girls tittered behind their hands at the sight of Miranda's bare face, whispering to each other, until Dorothea silenced them with a look.

Miranda stood in the center of the room, an ungainly doll, as they tied and straightened and cinched, preparing her for whatever new ritual came next. The girls worked behind her, intent on some complicated task involving Miranda's lower back, as Agata gave her commands. "Make your conversation lively and your replies gracious. Talk not of . . . where you've been. Speak of Prince Ferdinand and your happiness at being home. Remember every name, for I will ask you for them later." She tapped Miranda's waist. "There. Turn to the mirror, so you can see the lady you're meant to be."

Miranda made a stiff quarter-turn to the long, gilded mirror and saw they had made her into one of the pale women in the portraits. She was still not used to seeing her reflection in mirrors, having seen herself for so long only in ponds and puddles, and the image seemed uncanny. She almost imagined her arm left a ghost trail as she raised the sleeve of the rose-colored gown, trying to understand the relationship of this binding fabric to her body.

Dorothea interceded between Miranda and her double, holding a hinged wooden box in her hands. "Your father has sent a gift. From Venice." She lifted the lid of the box, and Miranda saw that it contained a full-face mask, the color of ivory, with gold and black ornaments around the eyes and a carmine moue on the lips.

Miranda lifted it from its box, and its black ribbons tumbled down. She held it before her face, and Agata nodded. "Keep it on all night. Do not remove it until you come back to these rooms."

"Why not?"

Agata's eyes flared. "Do as I say, girl. I know this castle far better than you."

Miranda slipped on the mask, accepting her fate. It allowed her more clarity than the veil, not covering her eyes, and she was grateful for that. Tonight she would watch, and meet the eyes of all those figures she had only witnessed as shadowy shapes, their faces sour with distaste. Perhaps she could make this mask her face; perhaps they would fall for her now, as Ferdinand had, and treat her like a human being.

Dorothea and the girls departed, though Dorothea threw Miranda one of her familiar winks as she slipped out of the room. Miranda and Agata sat in silence until Agata deemed it was time to go down to the celebrations.

The carnival ball splashed out across the courtyard of the ducal court, spilling into the surrounding halls and loggias. Men and women in masks darted in between the columns, shivering in the late-winter air, looking like fairies as the firelight played over their disguises, the greens and purples of their false faces glittering as if crafted from beetle wings.

Miranda stood above, looking out from the landing of the ducal apartments, afraid, suddenly, to descend into the festivities. They looked happier than she had ever seen them, the people of Milan, and she could not help thinking it was because she was not yet among them. She seemed to bring darkness here, no matter what she did: she oozed it, like pond mud.

"Well, come on." Agata took her arm, leading her down the stairs to where her father, maskless and clad in a long emerald coat, stood with several puffy-faced men. They nodded as she approached, and her father embraced her, introducing her to the counts of somewhere and some other place, who muttered to each other about this and that as she stood there, silent. They talked of plots in Pavia, of scandal in Savoy, of treachery in the Vatican, a place Miranda did not know but seemed, from what she could make out, to be filled entirely with old men who hated one another. She yearned for news of Naples, and of Ferdinand, but did not dare turn the conversation to the longed-for south. She did not ache to return to Ferdinand so much as to the sea: if only she could gaze upon its blueness, feel its briny breeze, she would be restored. She could live among these unfamiliar men for years, she felt, if only she could see the sea.

"Come, Miranda. Let us walk the courtyard. I leave for Galliate tonight before traveling to Lyon and have seen you so seldom since I regained my dukedom." Her father always spoke as if he were performing: it hadn't jarred Miranda when it was only the two of them, but now it seemed odd, an eccentricity she had not before registered. Prospero was triumphant tonight, taking no notice of the way the crowds parted around them, of the eyes boring holes through fine Venetian masks.

"Father, have you received word from Naples? From Ferdinand?"

"The Neapolitans dither over details, but they've promised to send word within the week. Don't fret, my child. The deed is done! You are restored to your castle, and I to my rightful place of power." He made an expansive gesture, taking in the carousal around them. "And how has it been? To be back among those who adore you so?"

Miranda was glad of the mask, for her mouth twisted beneath it. "They do not act as though they adore me, Father. They gawk, and they talk, and they hate the sight of my face."

That stopped him: he paused, drawing her close, turning away from the crowd. "It will take them time, Miranda. But you are their lady. Do not doubt it."

"But why do they ask me to cover my face, Father? And why do they speak of my mother to one another, but never to me?"

"Do not speak to anyone else of your mother." The command resonated, like a spell, and Miranda wondered if that was what his words were. He softened his tone, his hand on her arm. "If you have questions about your mother, come to me. I knew her much better than any of these others could. And I have talked to you of her often enough."

Once, Miranda thought. You spoke of her once, and only to unveil the grandeur of your own plans. But she drew a breath, said evenly, "Of course, Father. You knew her best, I'm sure."

He studied her with ice-blue eyes, and she feared that he would take offense and castigate her before the crowd. But he relented, saying only, "Heed not the words of lesser men. They envy your royal line and the wonder of your impossible return, as Caliban envied us our wisdom and wit, that inborn intelligence his sullied blood deprived him of." He guided her back into the crowd, presenting her to a clutch of well-dressed ladies with a flourish before bowing his way out of their company. "Forgive me, ladies. I must speak with the Spanish ambassador."

The ladies looked out at her from behind birdlike masks, and Miranda tried to embody her own mask's painted pout, to talk prettily of court intrigue and hunting seasons. But she faltered every time she went to speak and found herself moved from cluster to cluster, always on the outside of the circles, always watching the scene as though it were a shadow play.

Her mask felt tight on her face, and the heavy velvet and satin of her dress chafed and pinched. She felt like the phantom Milan treated her as, forced to witness the joy of the living but never to claim it as her own.

She found herself pushed to the very edge of the crowd and took refuge in the quiet of a loggia, watching pairs of young lovers dash beneath its shelter to exchange fervid kisses before laughing their way into the crowds again.

A hand descended upon her shoulder. She turned, expecting Agata, maybe even Dorothea: but the figure she saw resembled neither. It was tall, draped in black, and seemed neither man nor woman, its clothes shabbier than most of the court regalia. Upon its face, it wore a full mask: one that almost seemed to have been crafted from iron, thick and impenetrable.

She thought that perhaps she should be frightened, but she was used to strange sights, and though the stranger was a touch spectral, it emanated no menace. It stepped back from her, crooking a glove-covered finger, motioning for her to move down the hall, back into the interior of the castle.

Miranda followed, glancing back towards the party as she went. Had Dorothea, perhaps, prepared some surprise for her and enlisted the help of a friend to guide Miranda to it? The person kept looking back at her, and though she could not see its features, she felt it emanating concern, an attention to Miranda's presence she could feel from a few feet away.

"Who are you?" Miranda called quietly as they walked

the halls. "Did Dorothea send you?"

The figure made no reply. It was leading her, Miranda realized, to the portrait gallery. She trailed the figure up the steps, into the hall, where the old royals of Milan glowered in the half dark. Miranda stopped as the figure lumbered on, unwilling to get any closer to the shrouded portrait that had caused Dorothea pain. But the figure moved closer to the shroud, and then turned to Miranda, waving her forward. "I can't," Miranda pleaded, and she heard the stranger sigh: a rusty exhalation of breath, yet somehow light, familiar. It raised its thin arm, its hand hovering over the veil covering the portrait, and clutched its bony fingers around the fabric. She saw the shadow lift, and beneath, in the dim light, the shape of a face.

Her own face.

Miranda stood too far away to see the detail, ready at any moment to run, but there was no mistaking the pale woman captured in the painting's frame. Preserved in shades of coral and pearl, her own countenance looked out upon the portrait hall. She felt as though she were looking at her soul, stolen from her body and put up on the wall. She staggered back, closing her eyes to drive the vision from her mind.

"Miranda!"

Her name echoed bright and cheery down the hall,

like a summons from another world. A young man, dressed in a crimson suit and half-mask, emerged from around the corner. "I thought I saw you come this way. Come back to the ball! We don't want to be caught here again."

Miranda moved towards the dashing young man, who was not a man at all, but Dorothea a foot taller, her hair pulled back with a ribbon, her jawline heavier, a fine beard across her cheeks. "Dorothea? But . . . how?"

Dorothea pulled off her mask. "A glamour, of course. Your father must have used them, I'm sure. I wanted to dance with you at the ball! And while everyone fusses over the locations of young ladies, young men rove about as they please. I could be anyone's nephew from Orvieto, somebody's so-and-so from Verona. No one will question such a charming, lively young lad."

Miranda let out a laugh, and then caught herself, spinning back to peer into the gallery. The figure was gone. "Did you . . . send someone? To bring me here, so that we could meet?"

Dorothea scrunched up her nose. "Up here? No. In fact, I think we should get as far away from here as we can."

"But there was someone here, Dorothea. They showed me the portrait. The face that lies underneath the shroud—it's mine."

Dorothea's eyes went wide. "It can't be. It's been there since I came to this castle, Miranda. No one in Milan, in all of Italy, had seen your face since you were three."

"I promise you." She moved back towards the portrait, but Dorothea took Miranda's hand, pulling her back towards the ball.

"We need to leave this place," Dorothea urged. "And the portrait—" She stopped, squeezing Miranda's hand. "It can't be you, Miranda. It must be your mother."

"My mother?" She thought of the contours of the face, obscured by darkness. Perhaps the hair was a touch darker, the cheeks a bit thinner. Perhaps the face was not Miranda's own, but that of someone only a little older. "My mother."

"It makes sense. They say Beatrice was much beloved, and died too young, just before you and your father were banished from Milan. Twelve years later you appear again, looking exactly like she did when she was taken from this world. No wonder they call you a ghost."

"But why do they cover her face?" Here, in this castle she was meant to call her own, an image of her mother hung only steps from her rooms, and no one had told her. No one had taken her to look upon the face of the woman who had given her birth, who Miranda had lost before she knew the word "mother." Not even her father. Her eyes grew hot with tears, and she dropped Dorothea's hand, turning away.

"Miranda . . ." She felt Dorothea's hands on her shoulders. "I'm sorry. I am. I wish I could tell you why." Miranda let herself turn and accepted Dorothea's embrace. They stood, forehead to forehead, as Dorothea held her. "We must return to the ball. Agata will notice if you don't join the dancing."

"I don't feel much like dancing."

"I know." Dorothea rubbed small circles along her back. "But you can't stay here in the dark. You deserve a little joy, Miranda. Both of us do. Leave your worries for a moment and come dance with me. Please?"

Dorothea's new form was strong and radiated warmth. Miranda longed to stay in her arms, but she pulled back, accepting Dorothea's hand and letting herself be led away from the gallery. As they walked, she took a sidelong glance at Dorothea, at the handsome profile of her face. "Why did you change your sex? Do ladies not dance together?"

Dorothea tossed back her head, laughing. "Maybe in certain quarters of the city they do. But not in the ducal court." They were approaching the ball, the roar of the crowd reaching them as they walked towards the courtyard. "There are some courtly dances where it wouldn't seem amiss for two ladies—noblewomen, mind you, not foreign serving girls like me—to dance hand in hand in a group. But the first dance is for partners, and I want you to be mine."

They came to a landing overlooking the courtyard. Dancers were taking their places, and as the music began they moved in unison, their steps perfect, their every turn and twist precisely matched. Miranda clutched Dorothea's hand. "I can't do that! Dorothea, I've almost never danced before, much less danced like this. They're beauteous! They're marvelous! They're—"

"Stop, stop." Dorothea was laughing again, covering her mouth with her other hand. "These are the entertainers, Miranda. They've been practicing for weeks. Well, some of them are nobles, here to show off, though they pretend no one recognizes them behind their masks. See that man there?" She pointed to a young man in gold and blue, as tall and graceful as a swan. "He's the marquis of Mantua. He lives for this. The girls say he never does anything but dance, drink, and sleep. Not a bad life, eh? They'll dance for a while, and then they'll open up the floor for the rest of us. Don't fret, my lady." She raised their linked hands, motioning for Miranda to turn. "Let me show you the steps."

They went through the dance as best they could, with Dorothea telling her where the other couples would stand, and on which beat they would come together, and when they would break apart. Miranda tripped over her own feet once or twice, but with Dorothea's hand in hers she felt she could follow the rhythm, the little hops and circling steps. She thought of the spirits of the isle, of the way they pranced and strutted, and mimicked their movements as she clasped her hands behind her back, kicking lightly on her feet.

Dorothea grinned. "You see? I knew you could dance. I'm never wrong about these things." She glanced over the balcony and then extended her hand to Miranda. "And it's time for us to join the crowd. Are you ready?"

Miranda accepted Dorothea's hand. "As ready as I will be."

They plunged into the revelry and took their places in the square. Miranda swallowed, afraid of the eyes on them, afraid they would see Dorothea for who she was, but around them the crowd clapped and carried on, caught up in its own exuberance.

The musicians started up, and Miranda swung her way into the song, following the patter of Dorothea's feet, pinching her skirts and spinning, as the other ladies did. She and Dorothea circled each other, eyes shining through their masks, and Miranda felt her breath pick up, her heartbeat excited by the dancing. By the dancing, and by Dorothea, so near. Her smiling face was the center Miranda orbited as she let the music carry her, feeling free for the first time since she came to Milan.

They came together, holding their clasped hands aloft, and another couple passed beneath the bridge they'd made. The music pounded on, and on, and on, and Miranda felt her temperature rise, sweating against the cool winter air.

Giddiness rose in her, and she fell into Dorothea's arms at the end of the dance, the crowd erupting in joy. "Not bad for your first time," Dorothea whispered, grinning wide, and Miranda pushed herself up, the heat in her limbs suddenly unbearable. She pulled up her mask, drawing her hand across her brow in relief; and then she stopped, hearing the chatter around her falter.

A nearby clutch of gray-haired ladies fixed their glittering eyes on her naked face. One covered her masked mouth with her hands; the others, barefaced, let their jaws hang open, eyeing her with a hungry, fearful awe. She heard a gasp, from one of the women: "*Bice.*" And then repeated, like an incantation, an avowal, passed from tongue to tongue: "*Bice. Bice.*"

Miranda stood frozen, pinned beneath the women's gazes like a shrew sighted by birds of prey. Dorothea grasped her elbow, forcing her into motion, and she recovered enough of her sense to pull the mask back down. She looked past Dorothea's shoulder towards the staircase leading to the ducal apartments and saw Agata standing atop it, her eyes glinting silver as she watched the crowd. "Not that way." She swerved, steering Dorothea with a hand on her back. "I know another route."

"You found the tunnels!"

"I found the tunnels."

They moved swiftly, trying not to run, until Dorothea halted, nearly toppling Miranda to the ground. "Wait, take my mask," she urged, pulling off her own and handing it to Miranda. "Give me yours."

Miranda did as she asked. Dorothea grabbed the arm of a young woman they'd just passed, the cut of whose dress almost exactly matched Miranda's. The color was several shades lighter, but by candlelight it was hard to tell the two apart.

Dorothea thrust Miranda's mask into the lady's hands. "Marco told me it's your turn! We're all pretending to be the duke's daughter—this mask looks just like hers."

"The duke's daughter? The feral girl?" The woman began to laugh. She took the mask and traded it for her own, gurning at her companions. "Look, I was raised by wolves!"

"There are no wolves on—"

But Dorothea dragged Miranda away before she could expose herself. "Not now. Take shelter in the prejudice of these spoiled children and *run*."

"Who's Marco?"

"Who knows?" Dorothea winked. "But it'll keep Agata from searching for you. For a while, anyway."

They dashed on, weaving and winding through the ball until they reached the statue in the long deserted hall off the courtyard. Miranda glanced around and then ducked behind the base.

"Ready?" she whispered to Dorothea.

"As I'll ever be."

She pulled up the handle of the portal, and Dorothea followed her into the dark.

Chapter 4

They tumbled out of the tunnels into Miranda's rooms, letting themselves down onto the floor with as little injury as they could, for Miranda had not left a chair to catch them. "Can you do something to the door?" she asked Dorothea as they got to their feet. "A spell, in case Agata comes?"

"Even easier than that." Dorothea removed a slender key from the lining of her red jacket. Its edges had all been filed off, save for the hook at its end. "As good luck would have it, I borrowed this from the blacksmith just yesterday in exchange for brewing him a potion to provoke his performance."

Miranda wrinkled her nose. "He's in the theater?"

Dorothea laughed as she darted over to the door. "If so he's a poor player. But my concoction will soon have him strutting the stage."

Miranda watched her slide the skeleton key into the lock. "So it works on any door in the castle?"

"Most of them. I needed garments for the ball, and there's a heap of them stored away in this place."

Dorothea placed the key back in her inner pocket. "There. That'll keep Agata out, for a time."

They had been breathless with laughter and fear during their escape. Now, as they stood back in her prison, Miranda remembered the looks of the ladies at the dance who had seen her true visage. She knew now that her face matched her mother's, and she knew that this likeness was the cause of the whispers, the claims that she was no girl at all, but some wight brought to life by Prospero. Yet she still could not understand the revulsion this face alone inspired.

Though the mirror in Miranda's room unnerved her, she had spent an afternoon a few days past examining her face in its glass, trying to make out in the dim winter light whether her features matched those of the people she'd seen in Milan, in Naples, on the roads of Italy. Was she deformed in a way she had not perceived, as Caliban was? Yet thinking back on Caliban's face, she could not remember why his form held such repugnance: he limped, yes, but she had seen men here on land who limped, who held bronze-handled canes and carried their heads high. He was dark, but she did not see why darkness should signify corruption, now that she had beheld the wide range of human hues; broad-nosed, but she knew now that the faces of men were made of clay that could be sculpted into any shape. What had caused her to think Caliban so ugly a man, when, as she gazed upon her own reflection, it seemed to warp and waver, unsettling her so profoundly that she had to look away?

She pulled off Dorothea's mask, set it aside, and sat on the edge of the bed. Dorothea settled beside her. "Are you all right?"

"Dorothea, you've shown me such kindness. Kindness no one else has. But I think you've been less than honest with me. I ask you now, if you are my friend, to give me the truth as plain as you can. The way the others look upon my face—" She stopped, her breath catching in her throat. She did not cry often, but she could feel the tears building now. "Dorothea, there can be no other reason. I must be hideous, and terrible to look upon. Is there something wrong with my face, Dorothea? Something all of Milan can see, but I cannot?"

"Of course there isn't."

"Please don't lie to me, Dorothea. I cannot bear it."

Dorothea took both of Miranda's hands in hers, dipping her head to meet Miranda's downcast eyes. "Miranda, you're beautiful." When Miranda did not lift her gaze, Dorothea cupped her cheek gently. Their eyes locked, and Miranda trembled, her skin still cool from the winter air. "You don't know that, truly? You're a beauty to inspire sonnets. You're a beauty fit for a prince. Didn't Ferdinand fall in love with you at first sight?"

"But then he cast me aside. Maybe he was only under a spell. Maybe Father made him think—"

Dorothea pressed a finger to Miranda's lips. "No sorcerer could weave a spell this complete. I work with magic of just this kind: you've seen me change my face. No mage crafted this countenance, Miranda." Miranda felt a flush spread over her skin. "Eyes like this, dark and sparkling jewels, are rare enough that painters and sculptors both would struggle their whole lives to capture their reflection, were they lucky enough to glimpse them even once. And coming so close as this, drawn into your orbit, they would lose all ability to remember, to reason, to pick up the brush, to reach for the clay. Men would lose their art, for you." She ran her thumb lightly over Miranda's cheekbone. "If there is anything I find wanting about your face, Miranda, it is only that I long to gaze upon it in the sun, where it belongs."

Miranda's heart was pounding. Her body ached like it used to when she would stand at the edge of the eastern cliffs, daring herself to jump into the sea. She longed for Dorothea to keep speaking, for her words to rush on in their wonderful way. She longed for a reason to leap. "What else? Dorothea—what else?"

Dorothea's lips quirked into a smile. She was close now, close enough that Miranda could count the flecks of gold in her eyes. "They wouldn't write sonnets, now that

I think about it. Poets would sooner abandon their pens, for your beauty defies all verse. I cannot honor the perfection of your form with poetry, but with touch alone." She ran her fingertips over Miranda's ear. "I honor this nape of your neck, the curve of which would drive all artists mad. The silken strands of your hair. And your lips . . ."

"Yes?"

"Your lips . . ."

"Dorothea . . ."

"To honor your lips, my only tribute can be this."

Their mouths came together softly, sweetly. This was nothing like kissing Ferdinand. He and Miranda had exchanged a few furtive kisses, but no more. At the castle in Naples, they had been kept in separate rooms, and always their families were near. Here, for these moments, she and Dorothea were alone in the world. Miranda drank Dorothea in, reveling in the smell of sweat on her skin, the tug of her teeth on Miranda's lower lip. Dorothea was sand and sea, Miranda thought dizzily. She was wind and water and heat all at once, a tempest of her own making.

She brought her hand to Dorothea's cheek and felt it growing smooth beneath her touch. Dorothea was changing back, her glamour fading. Miranda's desire quickened as Dorothea's long hair tumbled from the ribbon that held it back, her lips regaining their rosy plumpness. Dorothea guided her back onto the bed, pressing Miranda into the pillows as she kissed her way down her neck, and Miranda gave herself over to her skilled hands. How good it felt, to stretch her body again. To use it the way she wanted.

Dorothea's hands traveled to Miranda's hips, tracing their outlines beneath her dress. Miranda shivered. Dorothea released her mouth from Miranda's collarbone and sank back onto her heels, straddling Miranda with a grin. Miranda blushed as their eyes met. "Dorothea, I don't know . . . that is, I'm not certain what—"

"Don't fret, my lady." Dorothea gave her one last lingering kiss before slinking down to lift Miranda's skirts. "Let me show you the steps."

～

Lying in Dorothea's arms afterwards, Miranda could hear the carrying on of the court. She could hear the music, as pleasing as birdsong. She could hear the cries and shouts, the effervescent clamor bubbling up through stone walls, a sign that the world outside spun on, not knowing how it had changed within this room. No longer did it vex her, for she felt part of the world now.

She could feel Dorothea's breath lagging, coming even and slow, but Miranda had no wish to sleep. She felt like she did after a long evening swimming at the beach, falling onto the dunes, sated and salty and spent, but still eager to watch the stars spin, to stay awake as long as she could. She nudged her nose into Dorothea's neck. "You may claim that poets go mute before me, but you're one yourself, you know. You charm with your words as well as with your spells."

Dorothea stroked Miranda's hair. "My mother wrote poetry. I used to translate it, to teach myself languages. From Arabic to Spanish to Italian and back again. 'Learn a language's poetry and you will know its soul.' That's what my mother always told us."

"I'd like to read her poems."

"Maybe I'll write them back down someday. But the original poems are gone."

"Gone?"

"Destroyed. The Spanish authorities heaped my mother's books on bonfires, along with all the Arabic writings they could find. When we came to Italy, we lost many more things, things we had to sell or things that others stole. And we kept losing them. When your home is not your own, it's hard to keep much. They were only parchment, anyway. I have them all memorized by heart, in three languages. She used to recite them to us at night, teaching us the verses. That, I cannot lose."

Miranda considered this. She knew so little of

Dorothea's life before Milan, of the journey that had brought her to this castle, and she was suddenly overwhelmed with the desire to know all her stories at once. "You told me that you changed your name."

"Hmm?"

"When you came here, to Italy. You said that you changed your name."

"I did."

"What's your real name, then?"

Dorothea was silent a long time. Then she sat up a little, dropping her hand from Miranda's head. "Duriya."

"Duriya." Miranda savored the sound. The taste of Dorothea on her tongue still flavored every word, coating it in honey. "It's pretty. Why did you change it?"

"Because it marks me as a Moor."

"What's a Moor?"

"The meaning changes as you move through the world. In some cities it's used for followers of Mohammed, in others a person from the northern reaches of Africa, settled now in Spain. Here it means almost anyone with skin darker than your own, with a name you can't pronounce."

"And it's a bad thing, to be a Moor?"

"It's a dangerous thing in this part of the world. To be a Moorish woman—well, that's worse. The men try to get you with a Christian child and tell you it's to save your own soul. The women might employ you for a time, but they'll throw you to the dogs to save their own skins if the inquisitors come knocking. I'm safest in these castle walls, where my skin's never too long in the sun."

"I didn't know."

"How could you? Unless your Caliban was a Moor."

"He . . ." Miranda cast her mind back. "His mother was from Algiers, and his skin was dark. Much darker than yours. So I suppose he may have been. But like me, he knew little of where he came from. We were both of the island. It was all we could remember."

"I see."

Dorothea's hand lay limp on the bed from where it had fallen from Miranda's hair. Miranda took it, tracing lines over the palm. "Would you prefer I call you Duriya?"

"No." Dorothea's lips were tight. She took a breath and then curled her fingers over Miranda's hand. "Call me Dorothea. For now. When others call me by my old name . . . it reminds me of my sister and brother. And my mother. It's painful, to know I'll never again hear it from her mouth. No one here can say it quite right, anyway. It hurts to hear your name said wrong, again and again. To be called something other than what you are, by people who don't even know what it is they're saying."

Miranda bit her lip. "I'm sorry." She felt as though she were walking through treacherous woods, unsure of her steps. "Why do you stay, then? Or why not wear the glamour? If it's easier to be a man, you could make yourself one."

"Where would I go? I don't wish to travel alone, disguised as a boy for the rest of my life. There is no place I know that seems much better, and there are many more I know to be worse. I don't wish to change my skin, and I cannot change my blood. And I can't go back to Marrakech. I don't want to marry, or struggle as my mother did."

"But surely, with your powers, you can live a different way? No one could stop you, could they, from living the life you choose?"

Dorothea pulled her hand from Miranda's grip. "I still need to eat. No witch can make bread from rocks alone. You may be heiress to riches untold, but all I have, I've gained for myself. I don't want to live in a cave, or only walk the world in darkness. I want to be in it. Part of it." She looked away. "I know you don't understand this yet, Miranda. I know it's all new. But to be in this world, you must always be a little less than yourself. With every day that passes, you must give up a little more. And . . . it hurts. If you dwell on it, it sometimes hurts too much to bear."

With that, the door to Miranda's prison seemed to swing shut once more. She swallowed the lump in her

throat, turning onto her back to stare at the celestial beings on the ceiling above. She was still unused to people,
to their moods and their depths and their secrets. The
spirits of the island were mercurial, but to them everything was a game. They acted because they were bound
or bored, not because of their histories or their passions.
Miranda had been treating Dorothea as though she were
a fairy guide, come to release her from her friendless exile. But these were people. Real people. And she had no
idea what to do with them.

Ferdinand was a real person, too. He had flitted
through her mind at that first kiss but vanished quickly
as she became caught up in Dorothea. Now his face reap-
peared in her mind, and with it the expression he might
wear, were he to stumble upon this scene. The sweetness
in her mouth turned to ashes. Was this the tang of betrayal on her tongue? Had she betrayed Ferdinand? She
could tell now, with the tension gone from her hands,
her hips, how angry she had been with him. Angry for
his silence, for his failure to send for her. Angry for the
promises he'd made and broken, and for her own naïveté,
for the way she had fawned over him when first he came
to her isle. Still, they were betrothed, and while she still
failed to understand exactly what that entailed, she was
certain this night with Dorothea did not fall within its
boundaries. She had wanted Dorothea, deeply, but she

had wanted to hurt Ferdinand, too, even if he never learned what had transpired. She wanted all these things, these contradictions, and she knew not which kind of wanting was right.

Guilt roiled in her gut. She could see Dorothea didn't care to talk further, but she had no one else to ask. She turned back onto her side. "Dorothea, do you think we—"

But her words were swallowed by the sound that came cascading through the room. A voice, filling every inch of the chambers. She and Dorothea locked eyes as Prospero began to address his subjects and his noble peers in the courtyard below.

"Heed me, people of Italy, for the false reign is ended. The righteous ruler is restored, bringing you a world glorious and renewed." The windows rattled with proclamation. "Though I have been a king in distant climes, I returned for you, Milan. Though I have been a god in exile, I yearned for you, Milan. I built paradise from an island untamed, but this country is my body, the love of my people is the blood in its veins, and I am its beating heart."

Dorothea had been wrong: Prospero's power was not contained in books alone. Miranda had heard that voice quake through the ground. She had seen it shake forests of aspen and rend groves of oak, and now it rang around them as though he stood in this very room, at the foot of their bed.

She sat bolt upright. Dorothea grabbed her hand.

"He kept it." Miranda's panic rose like a wave. "The power, Dorothea. The power he said that he renounced when we left. He has it still."

"Why, Miranda? Why does he cause his voice to echo that way?"

"To be heard throughout the castle." She closed her eyes. Her father's voice thundered on, promising an age of prosperity never before known in Milan, in all of Italy—nay, even the globe. "To be heard in its deepest tunnels."

"Why there?"

"He keeps my uncle there. Antonio." Dorothea's hold on her hand tightened. "He has him locked away, and he wants him to hear every word of this. There must be a reason, Dorothea. He must have plans unknown, plans beyond even taking back his dukedom." Her old fears, cast aside since she had come to the mainland, surged back as her father's speech came to a roaring, riotous close, the crowd bursting into applause that he amplified throughout the halls. He could appear at any moment. He could even catch her here, half-naked, tangled up in sheets with Dorothea. He could control her, and anyone in his reach, as easily as he once enslaved Ariel.

"Breathe." Dorothea's hand was on her chest. "Breathe deep, Miranda. You'll faint if you do not." She calmed a little beneath Dorothea's touch, though she still struggled to bring air into her lungs. "You must tell me what you know. You said someone brought you to the gallery, yes? What did they look like?"

"They were tall." She steadied her voice. "Thin. Far too thin."

"Starved."

"I couldn't tell. They wore a mask and covered every inch of their skin. I could not even tell if they were man, woman, or spirit beneath those clothes."

"I think it was your uncle, Miranda."

Miranda shook her head. "He's locked away. My father has him in a cell smaller than this bed."

"This castle has strange ways. A mind of its own, some say. Doors open when they shouldn't, and shut and lock, too. And your uncle was the duke a dozen years, ruling in peace. There are still those loyal to him, you know. If they've discovered where he's kept, he has friends in the castle who would aid his escape."

"If he was able to escape, why come to me?"

"Maybe there's something he needs you to know before he escapes for good. He wouldn't expect you to trust him." Dorothea's mouth pursed. "For some reason, he needed to show you the portrait of your mother."

"What could she have to do with this, Dorothea? She died long ago."

"But how did she die? What happened to her? Why do all the servants whisper her name? There is more to know, Miranda, and your uncle has the answers. Can you find your way back to where your father is keeping him?"

"Yes, but—" They froze at the knocking at the door. Miranda grasped Dorothea's hand. "Agata. It must be Agata."

Dorothea sprung up, gathering her clothes. She pulled the skeleton key out of her jacket and pressed it into Miranda's hands. "Wait a few moments and then let her in. Don't let her see the key. I'll come back through the tunnels tomorrow, as soon as night falls."

Together they ran to the tapestry, and Dorothea pressed a hasty kiss to Miranda's lips before Miranda helped hoist her into the portal.

"Miranda, open this door!" she heard Agata demand just as Dorothea's legs disappeared. Miranda steadied the tapestry and ran back to her bed, tugging on as many of her rumpled garments as she could manage. With trembling hands, she managed to unlock the door, slipping the key into her sleeve and backing away as quickly as she could.

Agata burst into the room. "I found the baroness of Carini climbing the terrace, making obscene animal noises, and wearing this." She thrust Miranda's mask onto the bed, advancing on Miranda. "Did I not tell you, above all else, to keep your face covered? For one night and one night alone, can you not pretend to be half the lady that your mother was?"

"And what kind of lady was she?" Miranda retorted.

Agata halted. "What did you say?"

"You knew her, didn't you? Tell me about her. Please. I don't remember her, and no one will tell me how she died. What happened to her, Agata?"

Pallor crept over Agata's face. "You will not ask." She turned on her heel and then spun back to snatch up the mask. "And you will wear the veil. Count yourself lucky that I allow you to go without it in your rooms. Try anything like this again, and I will fasten it to your scalp, I promise you. You may have lived like a pagan in your father's house, but you will not shame this castle."

She left Miranda shaking as the heavy lock fell into place on the door.

Chapter 5

The next day passed with agonizing lethargy. Miranda watched the weak rays of the sun slip across the floor, willing the shadows to lengthen, black night to fall once more. When it did, after the last of the servants left her alone in her rooms and the castle lay silent, Dorothea did not appear. Miranda waited in the dark. Had some task delayed her, or had Agata discovered Dorothea's role in last night's events and punished her? She knew nothing of the schedules of servants: How late did Agata make them work? How early were they required to wake, to do the whole day's labor all over again?

She had nearly given up hope when she heard a thumping at the portal. She leapt up and grabbed a chair, bringing it to the tapestry to aid Dorothea's descent. Dorothea's black hair had come loose from her bun in thick strands, and her face was smeared with dirt. "You must be careful that Agata doesn't discover you know of this portal, Miranda. I think she suspects. She set someone to wait by the statue of Virgil."

"How? And how did you get here?"

Dorothea dusted herself off. "She knows about the tunnels, of course. But she can't forbid you from using them, because that would acknowledge their existence, you see? She can't accuse you without revealing them. She must have guessed that you left the ball via Virgil's portal, since that's the entrance nearest to the courtyard. But the tunnels are deep, and they lead out of the castle itself. I got back in by taking the path that lets out in the woods, and I've explored as much as I could these last few hours. I wanted to make sure we had other ways to come and go."

"Did you see my uncle?"

"Not yet."

"Let's go. I can lead us there, and now's as safe a time as any."

Dorothea looked wistfully towards the bed. "All right. But I much prefer how we spent last night."

Together they made their way through the tunnels, trading little touches to reassure themselves in the dark. They came to the covered road, and Dorothea pointed. "There. If you keep going, you reach the exit. It brings you up in a ditch outside of the castle." Miranda could make out her wry smile in the torchlight as Dorothea took a flambeau from the wall. "Keep that in mind for the inevitable rebellion."

"Antonio's cell is this way." Miranda led her down the passage. "Do you know what used to be down here? The rooms in which he's kept look as though they haven't been used for years."

"Most people I know avoid the eastern part of the castle altogether, if they can." Dorothea shrugged. "Ghost stories. The girls say it's haunted."

"They believe everything to be haunted. This castle, the portrait, my face. On the island we could see the spirits. We didn't make up stupid stories to scare ourselves."

Dorothea started to laugh and then grew quiet. "Do you hear that?"

Miranda listened. A scraping sound, slow but ceaseless, echoed down the hall. "We're close," she told Dorothea in a low voice. "It must be him."

They came to the iron door, and Miranda guided Dorothea to the crevice looking into Antonio's cell. Dorothea angled the torch so that they could both see inside. Her uncle was pulling the chains against the wall, over and over. He lifted one wrist and let it drag down, down, down, scratching against the stone: and then repeated the action with his other hand, in unvarying rhythm. Dorothea knocked her fist against the door, two sharp raps, and he dropped his arm, the chain clattering to the floor.

"Hello, Antonio. We've come to talk." Dorothea stepped back, letting Miranda step forward so that Antonio could see her through the aperture.

Antonio stared. His eyes were as black as stones. Then he laughed, in a rasp that sounded like it pained him to release. "You were just here." His chest was bare, and she could see the scars etched across his sides. "Don't tell me there's more. I can't help you, and I can't help her, no matter what you say. Leave me in peace. Please."

Miranda looked at Dorothea. "He thinks you're someone else," Dorothea whispered. "Tell him who you are. Help him remember."

She turned back to the door, pressing her forehead against it, trying to show Antonio more of her face. "I wasn't here before. Or, I was, but—several nights ago. I saw you, but I wasn't sure if you'd seen me. It's me. Miranda. Prospero's daughter, whom you found on the island. Remember? With King Alonso and Prince Ferdinand and all the rest?"

"The rest." His words were slurred. "The rest, the rest. Do you know who was among the rest? Who rests there still?"

"I don't— Who, Uncle? Who do you mean?"

Antonio pulled on his chain. "I mean my son." He wound the links around his arm, in a way that it hurt her to watch. "My son, who your father drowned, *Miranda*. My son, who he forced me to forget until it was too late. Until long after we set sail and left that wretched place behind."

She glanced towards Dorothea. "Did he have a son?"

Dorothea shook her head. "No, his wife died in childbirth, or so I've heard. The baby died, too. His son never lived, Miranda."

Within his cell, Antonio snorted. "These lies he weaves, complete. He is a spider, and we but tortured flies."

"But Ferdinand said . . ." Miranda bit her lip. "On the island. When first we met. He told me that they had been shipwrecked, all of his party. The king of Naples, and the duke of Milan, and . . ." Ferdinand's voice cut through her memory clearly. "His son. Dorothea, Ferdinand spoke of Antonio's son, I'm sure of it! He said the duke of Milan and his son were both shipwrecked in the storm."

"He made me forget him." Antonio tightened the looped chain on his arm. "He made everyone forget him. Only I remember, and only once we returned home. He let me rave like a madman before the castle guards, and then he locked me away in this cell. He robbed me of the chance to save my son, my Alessandro, who my dear wife died to bring into this world, now dead himself and unburied, washed up on the shores of some godforsaken archipelago. It was not enough, to take my dukedom. He had to—" The chain dug into his flesh, and Miranda could see the red welt blooming beneath. "He had to have his revenge, you see? His true vengeance, bitter and dark and known to nearly none. Pay no attention to the play he puts on, to the fine words he speaks, for Prospero hides his devious designs better than any of us. Far, far better than me."

"Uncle, stop. Stop!" She pounded on the door, and Antonio released the chain. "You must be wrong. My father may be many things, but he is no murderer. He would never be so cruel as to make a father forget his child."

"What about a child his mother, then?" Antonio's eyes fixed on hers. "What about that Caliban? What did Prospero do to his mother, the witch?"

Her heart chilled. "Sycorax was . . . that was different. He didn't kill her. And she was . . ."

"She was what, Miranda?" She felt Dorothea's breath in her ear. "A witch?"

Miranda shook her head. "That's not what I mean."

"Witch or brother or child or beast," Antonio chanted, "it matters not. If Prospero counts you as his enemy, you are lost."

"It isn't true," Miranda whispered. "He's not . . . He was good. He was kind to me. He loved me, I know it."

"Love, in the heart of a man like that, is a terrible, twisted thing. His love warps. His love corrupts." Antonio got to his feet, chains draping from his arms. "His very love is a sin against God, my girl. The Devil would hand over the keys of Hell to Prospero, should your father offer his hand."

"You are a liar." Miranda's voice shook. "You lie to disguise your treachery."

"I do not claim to be a good man, child. I deserve my brother, as he deserves me. But my son deserved neither of us." Antonio looked towards the ceiling of his cell. "And Milan does not deserve Prospero, or the horrors he will wreak."

"What do you mean?"

"Think: your father had twelve long years alone on that isle to plot, to plan, to test the limits of his art. You know your father, Miranda. Better than any of us. Better than me, for I underestimated his power, fatally. When he did not return the fifth year, or the tenth, I thought myself safe. I thought Milan safe. What do you imagine he has come back here to do? He was never interested in politics or diplomacy. His interests lie in a realm far darker and more dangerous."

She heard Dorothea's voice in her ear, quiet but urgent. "We shouldn't stay much longer, Miranda. Ask him. About the gallery, and the portrait. About why he brought you there."

Miranda pressed her hands to the door, steadying herself. "Uncle, you came to me at the ball, didn't you? To show me the portrait of my mother?"

From where he stood, she could no longer see his eyes for the shadows. "Your mother."

"Yes—in the gallery? Her face looks like mine. Is that what you meant to show me? Is that why you escaped?"

Silence. She met Dorothea's eyes. "You remember her, don't you?" Her voice echoed through the lonely cell. "Beatrice? Bice?"

Her uncle made a sound then, a kind of keening. His body contorted, and he folded in on himself, his lank hair falling across his face, his chained arms over his head. "You must not be told. He said—she said—never. Never tell the child. She must never know."

"Who said I must not know? My father is gone, to Galliate, and then to Lyon. He won't return for days. You can speak freely, Uncle. Tell me why you brought me there."

"Miranda—" Dorothea was tugging at her dress.

"I cannot speak. He hears! He hears! Every word, he hears."

"Miranda, listen. Someone's coming!"

Underneath her uncle's moans, she heard it. From the darkness outside the rooms in which they stood. A clicking, like bones on stone. Antonio's cries grew louder, and he began to shake his chains, collapsing in a heap beneath them.

"It comes! It comes! He sends, and it comes, and we are lost, all lost, for Hell is here! Prospero has plundered Heaven, and its riches rot around us."

"We must go." Dorothea pulled Miranda from the door. "He cannot tell us anything. We have to find a different way."

They turned and ran, the sharp, steady tapping following them down the empty tunnels as they sought the refuge of Miranda's rooms.

~

Back in her chambers, Miranda paced the floor. She dared not reignite the dying fire and so could only see Dorothea's face by the moonlight that streamed through the windows, giving her skin a ghostly, etiolated sheen. Miranda longed for the comfort of the night before, before they had opened this Pandora's box and unleashed these mysteries. She did not know how to reconcile Antonio's wild tales with what she knew of her father.

What frightened her most was one persistent, pernicious thought she could not put out of her mind, one repeating line. Her father was a story he had told her himself. Everything she knew of his deeds and motivations came straight from his own mouth. And now that she knew he had lied about surrendering his magic, a vow as solemn and binding as any she could imagine, she could not help but wonder what other falsehoods he had dressed as truth.

"He won't talk." Dorothea's voice startled her out of her contemplation. "He's petrified. We need a different way to find things out."

"How, Dorothea? I cannot ask my father, and no one else will teach me my history or speak of the reasons for our exile. What do they fear? Whence comes such silencing terror?"

"We don't have to ask." Dorothea's eyes gleamed. "I know of magics for walking in minds, Miranda. Dream magics that allow a traveler to slip in and out of nighttime visions, leaving the dreamer none the wiser. I could do it, I think. It's difficult and a little dangerous. But you need to know what your father and the others are hiding from you."

"You don't have to help me, you know." Miranda formed the words gently on her tongue, for she spoke with real concern, but they left her lips biting. She cleared her throat. "I mean—this is not your burden, Dorothea. My father's machinations, my mother's fate: I do not wish these things to consume you. I am born to this dark plot, but you can walk away."

Dorothea shook her head. "I won't, Miranda. If what your uncle says is true, it's not only you in danger. It's all of Milan, and maybe the world beyond." She sighed. "Though it's my feet in the fire if we're discovered. The authorities would never harm the duke's daughter, and I believe your father would protect you in the end. But your Moorish accomplice, the heretical witch—"

"I know." Miranda imagined Agata's smiting hand, recalled the bruise blossoming on Dorothea's cheek. "We'll be careful. And I won't let them hurt you. I promise."

Dorothea's lips quirked. "You overestimate your influence with the men of Milan, my Miranda." She reached out, threading her fingers through Miranda's own. "But I care about you. I wouldn't leave your side, not now."

"Nor I yours." So it was decided. No matter how treacherous the path, she and Dorothea would see this through. "Tell me more of this magic, then. Surely my father would know at once if we used such a spell on him."

"He would. And Antonio, too, for his mind is unwilling, and his sleep these nights surely fitful. The spell works best upon an unguarded mind, one at relative peace." She tapped her finger against her lips. "We need someone who remembers. Someone who knew your mother and saw Prospero expelled from Milan. Someone who knows this castle like the back of their hand. Someone like—"

"Agata."

"Agata," Dorothea agreed. "She remembers, I'm sure of it. It has to be her."

"And you're certain she will not know that we walk in her dreams? That she will have no reason to suspect?"

"She abhors magic, Miranda. She would attend Mass every hour, if she could, and she believes her piety protects her from all interference. She'll have no idea. But we will need some of her things. A lock of her hair, and something she keeps near her as she sleeps. I'll need to gather mugwort and vervain for the potion, too, and a tincture of opium. The ingredients won't be hard to find, but I'll need to go outside the castle to get them."

"How long will it take you?"

Dorothea furrowed her brow. "Two days' time, should everything go smoothly. We can perform the spell the night after next."

"We must act as quickly as we can, as my father is due to return in a week. If he uncovers our plan—" Miranda quivered as she thought of the strange drowsiness that often overtook her on the island, of the swift consequences that befell her whenever she interfered with her father's plans.

"He won't," Dorothea promised. "He'll never know, Miranda. This is the safest way to draw out the truth." She took Miranda's other hand, tightening her grip. "But I can't enter Agata's rooms. If she discovers me, I'm doomed. She sleeps only three doors down from where we stand. Collecting what we need from her falls to you."

Shivers ran down Miranda's arms. "I—" *I don't want to,* she wanted to say. *I'm afraid. Please do it for me.* But she could not ask Dorothea to be her instrument, to risk her own life while Miranda remained ensconced in gilded chambers. She closed her eyes, imagining the journey to Agata's rooms. It would only be a few steps to Agata's door, but she would have to walk them exposed and alone.

Once upon a time the task would hardly have daunted her. She had scaled the island's highest cliffs and delved into the perilous caves in its deepest depths, with their knife-sharp rocks and slippery sides. She had roamed wild, even though her father's presence hung heavy over the beaches and the forests she traveled, even though she feared he might appear around every new bend on the wooded trails. On the island, though, the sun and stars had guided her; the sea and spirits had murmured around her, and she had felt the world was wider than even her father's influence, that beyond the edges of his power some greater plan prevailed. Here, in his castle, she could feel no higher law.

"How?" She clutched Dorothea's palms. "If she finds me, I may not be beaten, but I'll never again leave these rooms. She'd never let me."

"I'll slip a sleeping draught into her evening wine," Dorothea answered. "That'll be easy enough. And then tomorrow, as soon as the bells in the tower chime midnight, you'll go to her rooms and use my key to enter. She'll sleep as soundly as if she were dead. Take a few strands of her hair and something small from beside her bed. A trinket she won't notice missing."

Miranda swallowed. "All right. I'll do it. But you're certain it will work? That she will not stir, should I step across her threshold?"

"I'm sure." Dorothea smiled, though the usual crinkles around her eyes did not appear. "Get some sleep. I'll take care of everything else we need tomorrow."

Miranda entwined her fingers in Dorothea's grasp.

"Will you stay? Just for a little while. I don't think I'll sleep, should you go."

"I don't dare, Miranda. If we're discovered—"

"We won't be." Miranda bent to press a light kiss to Dorothea's lips. "Stay a little while. No one will know, as long as you leave before the sun rises."

"I'll stay an hour," Dorothea conceded. "An hour, and no more."

But in the end she stayed until the dawn, slipping out in the eoan light. Their hearts beat too fast from the chase, their bodies pressed too close, and Dorothea's nearness proved too tempting. After learning all the uses that beds could serve, Miranda wasn't certain she would ever sleep again.

Chapter 6

Miranda did not see Dorothea at all the next day. As her rooms darkened, night sapping the sunlight from every surface, her dread grew stronger. One of the servants she had seen before, a meek girl with furze-colored hair, came to prepare her chambers for sleeping but scurried off as soon as Miranda tried to speak to her. Miranda meant to discover if the girl knew where Dorothea was tonight, if Agata had taken the customary wine with her evening meal, but there was no way to know.

When the girl was gone, Miranda rose from her bed and changed from her nightclothes into the simplest shift she could find in her wardrobe, a garment that might pass as a servant's at a glance. She combed her fingers through her long hair so that it hung before her face, hoping that the halls would be almost empty at this hour, and that the shadows might act as her shroud.

Dorothea had tucked the key into the space between Miranda's wooden bed frame and mattress, and as she reached to retrieve it she felt a now-familiar sensation on her skin, a phantom breeze that raised the fine hair on her arms. She turned, half expecting to see the door pushed open and Agata standing there, but it was shut. Her hand closed around cold metal, and she pulled the key from its hiding place. She let it rest for a moment in her palm, taking a deep breath, and then moved towards the door, which opened easily as Miranda inserted the key in its lock.

Outside her chambers, nothing stirred. She stepped gingerly, fearful of her echoing footfalls on the stone floor. As she passed the door to her father's rooms, she paused mid-step before remembering that his chambers were empty, that he was far from the castle. He had no Ariel to spy for him here, and he would not return from France for days.

She came to Agata's door and unlocked it before she could think better of it. She eased it open with the barest creaking and crept inside, pulling it shut behind her.

Agata slept in chambers far more austere than Miranda's own. Her bed was simple and small, and the gilded trinkets and sumptuous touches adorning Miranda's rooms were absent. In the dim moonlight, Miranda could make out some details of the paintings Agata had hung in place of the grand tapestries she had seen elsewhere in the castle. There was a man with long dark hair and hollow eyes who reminded her a little of Antonio, whose hands bore marks as though the palms had been pierced straight through. She thought that he might be the man on the cross in the Duomo, and the woman in blue in the next portrait his mother. Their gazes seemed to linger on her as she walked towards the bed, where Agata lay on her side, her face turned to the window.

As Dorothea had promised, Agata slept soundly, dead to the world. On her pillow Miranda found a few loose strands of hair and threaded them around her fingers, breathing a sigh of relief. While she trusted Dorothea's magic, she'd been dreading the thought of plucking hair from Agata's head, for she could imagine Agata's thin fingers closing around her wrist, could picture her dark eyes burning as she awoke to find Miranda violating the sanctity of her chambers.

She stood for a moment, watching Agata sleep. In repose, Agata looked happier than Miranda had ever seen her, at far greater peace. The deep lines around her mouth and eyes had smoothed, and she looked ten years younger. Miranda could almost imagine Agata waking and greeting her with kindness, acknowledging Miranda as her kin, for Miranda could see now how much Agata looked like her mother. She longed for Agata to rise and embrace her, to tell her that she had been wrong to treat Miranda with such cruelty, that she and all the citizens of Milan were overjoyed to have Miranda home.

She turned away from the woman and her own foolish

thoughts. Near the bed she saw a chest of drawers and bent to examine its contents. She could take something small, something Agata wouldn't miss, and be on her way. In the top drawers she found instruments for sewing, several long strings of beads with crosses hanging from them, and a thick sheaf of papers, bound with a cardinal ribbon. Miranda drew the papers out of the drawer and squinted at the looping script. They were letters, she saw. Letters addressed to her.

Miranda stared at the letters, uncomprehending. *My dearest Miranda. My beloved Miranda.* She flipped fumblingly through the pages, her fingers gone numb. *We await you in Naples. We ask your father to send you as soon as he's able. I remain steadfast, my maiden mistress. My queen. My faithful wife.*

The adoring pronouncements, in Ferdinand's hand, blurred before her eyes. Agata couldn't have concealed messages from Naples from Prospero. She must have acted at his command. Her father had lied to her, from their very first days in Milan. Her father, who had brought them together. Her father, who kept her in this castle, against Ferdinand's wishes.

Her father clearly owed no fealty to Naples, or truly feared their king. Why, then, had he brought her here to rot? What did he intend by locking her away behind these walls, by separating her from Ferdinand?

Behind her, the bed creaked as Agata shifted in her sleep. Miranda shut the drawer quietly and left with the letters in hand, not caring if Agata noticed their absence. They were hers. They were proof that she had allies beyond these walls. Though all Milan might be against her, she still had friends in Naples.

Chapter 7

Miranda read the letters until the sun rose, and then for an hour or so after. When the knob of her door rattled, she snatched them up and hid them behind her back but relaxed when she saw that it was Dorothea.

"What have you got there?" Dorothea closed the door behind her, crossing over to Miranda. "Did you take those from Agata's rooms?"

Miranda nodded, holding the letters out before her. "They're from Ferdinand. He's waiting for me. He wants me to come to Naples as soon as I can. My father's been lying to me ever since I arrived."

Dorothea took the pages from Miranda's hands. "So Agata has been intercepting these."

"Yes." Miranda crossed her arms, suddenly feeling cold. "He's keeping me in his fortress, Dorothea. The marriage, the future he promised me, that he promised Ferdinand—it was an illusion. He doesn't want me to leave this castle."

Dorothea kept her eyes on the letters, looking through the stack. "It seems so."

Miranda examined Dorothea's face. She was not yet adept at reading emotions, but she was coming to know Dorothea's expressions as intimately as she had once known Caliban's, who always twisted up his mouth the same way Dorothea was now doing just before he began to excoriate Prospero. "Are you angry? Why are you angry?"

Dorothea turned away, laying the letters on the table. "We have to get you ready. I'm to dress you in the veil and send you to walk in the courtyard while I clean. Agata's waiting."

"Dorothea . . ."

Dorothea walked to the wardrobe, pulling out a green garment and bringing it over to Miranda's bed. "Your prince has sent for you. You should wear your fine gowns if you are to be queen of Naples." Dorothea's hands slipped over the folds of the dress as she straightened it out. "As you were meant to be. As you've longed to be."

"I want . . ." Miranda bit her lip. "Dorothea, I don't know what all of this means. I'm no queen, not yet. But when I am, I can curb my father's power, if he intends any evil. My time in Milan has been a misery, as you know well. Ferdinand can help me escape, and in Naples, I can make a new life."

Dorothea laughed, a short, ugly sound. "So you distract yourself from your troubles in Milan with the servant girl." Her fists tightened around the fabric. "I should have known I was only a new face to you. You've seen so few."

"Dorothea—"

"Get dressed." Dorothea still did not look at her. "We should not provoke Agata's anger today. I'll return at nightfall to perform the spell."

She helped Miranda dress in silence, her fingers moving over Miranda's hips and back as though she did not know their shapes. Miranda stared out the window at the gathering clouds, taking in one last view before Dorothea lowered the veil over her eyes.

~

That night, rain began to fall. Miranda lay in darkness, waiting for Dorothea. When she heard the thumping against the door from the tunnels, not long after she had gone to bed, she rose slowly, clutching the key in her hand.

They did not speak as she helped Dorothea down. Dorothea carried a small pouch, tied to her skirt, which she laid open on the table and unpacked as Miranda lit a lamp for her to see by. "Mugwort. Vervain. Opium. Do you have the rest?"

Miranda nodded and took the strands of Agata's hair

from where she'd stored them in one of her chests, along with the letters. She brought them to Dorothea, who placed a bottle on the table and began to mix the potent potion together, starting with the black strands of Agata's hair.

"Take one of these and burn it." Dorothea gestured to the letters. "We'll use the ash."

"What about the ribbon? Can I burn that instead?"

Dorothea's mouth tightened. "Fine. But work fast."

Miranda crouched before the fireplace. The ribbon hung limp in her hands. She fed its end into the fire, where it slowly caught flame, and let it burn itself out on the brick. The scorched portion left behind the lingering smell of burning hair and a dark, gritty powder, which she gathered up in her hands and brought to Dorothea.

"Pour it in." Dorothea held out the bottle, and Miranda added the ashes to the murky mixture. "After we take this, we'll fall asleep within minutes. As we sleep we'll be drawn to Agata's dreams. It may be hard to find our way at first. We'll have to cross the gulf between this world and the dream realm. But I've guided myself through trances before. If we—" She cleared her throat. "If we keep our hands together as we sleep, we'll walk together. Let me lead, and we will see all that Agata knows."

Miranda nodded. "Dorothea—thank you. For helping me."

"I could hardly do otherwise, my lady."

"Don't call me—" Miranda drew a breath. "Never mind. Are you finished?"

Dorothea held the potion aloft, its pinkish contents swirling in the half light. "Yes. And the fresher the better, so we should drink it now." She uncorked the bottle, taking a long sip, and passed it to Miranda. "Mind the hair."

When the bottle was drained, they made their way to the bed. They lay apart, not touching, until Miranda felt the draught take its effect. The sleep that stole over her was not unlike the dullness that had engulfed her so often at the island, a languor she now knew to be artificial. She risked a glance at Dorothea and saw her eyes were closing. "Dorothea," she whispered. "Take my hand."

Dorothea turned her head and stretched her hand out towards Miranda as though reaching across a chasm. Miranda caught her fingers and pulled her close, bringing their bodies together, just before they dropped into black and total sleep.

~

Full fathom five thy father lies.

Miranda opened her eyes. She could see nothing, but the voice of the void rang with familiar tones. It sang to her, and she relaxed into its embraces, her formlessness of no concern, her niggling sense of apprehension fading fast as the euphonic song lilted on.

Full fathom five thy father lies; of his bones are coral made. Those are pearls that were his eyes. The voice stopped and then began to speak, no longer singsonging its ghastly rhymes. "I thought of drowning your father many times. I thought of the look on his face as I forced him deeper and deeper down. As the water flowed into his lungs. I thought of his lifeless eyes so often that I saw them whenever I looked into his face, these last few years. His dead eyes, his blue pearls. I dreamed of it all the time, girl. Nothing brought me such pleasure as to imagine Prospero dragged down to the seabed, writhing and gasping like a fish on land. I dream of it still, though you both are gone. I dream of it still, and maybe someday my dreams will be real."

Miranda let the words roll over her, and then the meaning began to penetrate. "You dreamed of drowning him."

"Yes."

"You dreamed of drowning him . . . Ariel."

"Well done, little mortal." The voice gave a laugh like chimes. "Most who attempt what you are trying forget who they are, and their minds seep out like sand. But you're used to slipping into the void, aren't you? Your father made you visit it often. All those little grains of you, lost in the wind. Each time he sent you sleeping I wondered how long you'd last. I wondered when the time would come that you would no longer wake, or when you'd wake but would not see or speak." Ariel grew louder, his voice encircling her, ringing in her ears. "And so why, why, little mortal, would you bring yourself here? You survived. You stayed intact. Now the blackness will take you, and you will never, ever go back."

Miranda felt the greedy, gulping darkness tug at her from all sides. Not even darkness: the absence of any color, any light, any form. It would swallow her whole. "Ariel," she begged. "We wish to walk the dreams of a woman who knew my mother, long ago. We wish to discover why my father was forced from Milan and came to your island. If he has sound reason for his deeds, if he acted without cruelty, I cannot aid you in your revenge. But if my father is what you think he is, if he's sinned in some way, I'll help you, I promise. I will be your vassal in vengeance, with all the power of Naples behind me. I swear to you."

"And the other?" Ariel's voice snaked through her mind. "This little witch here, holding your hand. You want to keep her, too?"

Miranda's heart seized up as she realized she could no longer feel Dorothea's warm touch. "Yes! Please, Ariel. Deliver us into Agata's dreams, and back again."

"I can take you into the woman's mind, but you would have to find your own way back. And these waves are wine-dark and wanting. Demons wait to catch the unwary as they pass through. This is where I wait to pull your father down, should he ever come walking my way. If you say the word now, I'll take you and your sorceress back to your warm bed instead."

Miranda's mind raced. She could return and appeal to her father. Ask to be sent to Naples, with all she now knew. Perhaps she had misunderstood, and he had kept the letters from her for some less sinister reason. Perhaps he had only wanted to surprise her. But even as she tried to convince herself, she knew none of it could be true. She knew Prospero. Better, as Antonio said, than maybe anyone still living, other than Caliban, other than Ariel. She knew him, and she had to know the truth.

"Take us there."

"You're certain?"

"Take us there, Ariel."

"Very well." The spirit breathed out a sigh. "Humans never listen. It matters not if you tell them lies. They always put the truth aside."

Miranda felt the darkness shifting. She was moving, or the void was, and a whisper of touch—Ariel, maybe, or the faint press of Dorothea's fingers, back in the waking world—passed through her. "Wait. I pray you, Ariel, just one last question before I go."

"Yes?"

"Are you with Caliban?"

"I am. He's stopped cursing me, for your father has stopped cursing him. The island is peaceful. We live without masters now."

"That's good." Miranda tried to smile but found she had no face. "Tell him . . . tell him I'm sorry. I didn't understand."

"I will tell him." The void churned, and Ariel's voice slipped farther and farther away from her, echoing in the nothingness. "I will tell him. I will tell him."

The refrain faded, and Miranda heard no more.

Chapter 8

"Bice!"

Beatrice did not slow. She was far across the hills, and Agata struggled to keep up. Bice's legs had always been longer, her gait more assured. She strode where Agata straggled, and her strong, tanned limbs carried her across the green expanse easily even with Miranda in her arms, tucked against her bosom as she carried the apples they'd already picked in a swinging basket in her other hand.

Beatrice's skin freckled brown in the sun, and she would do nothing to protect it, which had caused Agata's aunt no end of consternation in their youth. The portrait of Beatrice recently hung in the castle's gallery painted her skin as smooth and creamy as milk. Her true skin was dappled with spots though she had barely reached her twentieth birthday, her face already grooved with lines from lounging about outside and from laughing. She laughed often, Beatrice did. Or at least she had, until these last few months.

It was unfair, Agata thought as she caught up to her cousin, that all these flaws only served Beatrice's beauty.

She had always looked a touch wild, like a mare who couldn't be broken. Now, as a young mother, she looked like a goddess, her dark hair flowing down her shoulders, her teeth gleaming white as she bit into a crisp red apple.

"Mm." Beatrice chewed, spitting out seeds as she went. "They're even better this year! It's the cold, I think. Made them tastier."

"We can't eat them all out here. Giuseppe promised to make an apple tart this evening."

"We won't! Well, at least I don't think we will." Beatrice slipped a small knife out of the pouch tied to her skirt and cut off a piece of the apple to give to Miranda. Miranda chewed thoughtfully as her mother spoke. "In truth, I don't wish to return. Can't we stay here, Agata, and start an orchard of our own? We could live in a simple shack and sell fruit on the road to Como. If I ran away, would you join me?"

Agata sighed. "Don't be foolish, Bice." She lifted an apple from her own basket. "Have you spoken to him?"

"We've spoken." Beatrice scraped her teeth over the core. "We've spoken, and still he persists. I do not think he hears me anymore, Agata. Truly. I think all he hears are the voices in his head. No one can reach him. Not me, not Antonio. Not even Miranda can persuade him to stop his work."

Agata looked down at the little girl, who had cocked

her head at the sound of her name. Everyone else said that Miranda had Bice's eyes, her ears, but Agata could only see Prospero in her face, in the defiant jut of the lip, her hooded eyes. It wasn't the girl's fault, but Agata couldn't help but resent her for the change she had brought to their lives, and to the castle. All this trouble began with her conception, three years before.

Prospero and Beatrice had been married a year before the pregnancy, and happily. Bice's parents were thrilled when the duke of Milan had taken an interest in their last surviving child after coming to tour their famous vineyards and had urged the match on, despite the reservations of their neighbors in Franciacorta, far from the city's walls. Perhaps the duke was eccentric, as they said, and a touch withdrawn, but on his arm their daughter would be a duchess. No strangeness in his nature could surmount that fact.

They had sent Agata along with her to Milan, to help Beatrice manage the castle and because Bice and Agata had been inseparable their entire lives. Though they were cousins, they called each other "sister," for Beatrice's parents had raised Agata after her own parents died in the fire that had claimed her childhood home. Their families had faced far too many tragedies, but now their fortunes were changing. Perhaps, they hinted, Agata would win the heart of the duke's unmarried younger brother, the dashing Antonio. She was plain, it was true, and growing older, but she favored Bice around the eyes a little, or maybe it was the mouth. "Be charming," her aunt had told her, "and attentive. Maybe your piety will impress him. They say though he is proud, he is devout, while the duke has not set foot in a church for a decade or more."

Agata had not needed urging, for she had fallen for Antonio at first glance. He was lean and muscled, stalking the castle like a wildcat, his black hair shadowing the sharp lines of his face. When he drank too much, which he did often, his cheeks flushed pink, and he would push his hair back, the shock of his dark unguarded eyes almost too much for Agata to bear. They worked closely together, tending to the many concerns of the castle that Prospero neglected, and talked often, though not nearly as often as Agata would have liked. She shadowed his steps like a younger sister, and he repaid her with all the grudging affection that relationship entailed.

Nothing she did swayed him, for Antonio had eyes for no one but Bice. He had never said it, but he didn't need to. She'd seen the look before. Countless men looked at Bice that way. And if Prospero ever extracted himself from the spirit world and took note of the way his brother looked upon his wife, he would see it, plain as day. Agata knew that would never happen. Prospero's blue eyes were clouded with visions from beyond this world. This palace, the people in it, were mist to him. If all of Milan drifted away as he worked, Agata was not certain he would miss it.

"Has Antonio appealed to him?" She turned her attention back to Bice, who was staring out at the first orange rays of the soon-setting sun. "If anyone can stop him, it must be Antonio. Has he tried?"

Beatrice scrunched up her nose. "Antonio will do nothing but what he wants, and he wants Prospero to keep himself locked away, so he can run the dukedom as he pleases. He wants Prospero to remain ensconced in his work and never again attend to matters of state. I know what Antonio wants."

Not all of what he wants, Agata thought, but she bit her tongue. Beatrice had never understood the power she wielded over men. She had mostly ignored their fervent attentions until the duke came along. She had been fascinated by his stories, his research, and his travels. They had spent hours together that first year, hours poring over the books in his libraries, hours discussing the true aims of alchemy and the building of a better world. It turned Agata's stomach, for such talk reeked of sacrilege. It was not for man to reshape the world and its workings, but for God alone. She told Bice as much, and Bice rolled her eyes. "It's hardly an affront to the Father, Agata. He changes metals into other metals and searches for new cures to old ills. There are alchemists with other aims, those seeking immortality, those craving unholy powers, but Prospero is not one of them. His art is harmless."

But then Beatrice's belly had begun to grow, and Prospero had become obsessed with the origin of the creature within. "Man creates life easily and yet understands little of its genesis," Agata had heard him say to Bice. "What man can make, he can understand. What he can understand, he can command."

He withdrew into his work as Agata tended to Beatrice's needs, as she prepared the ducal apartments for the coming of the baby. Agata had hoped Miranda's arrival might prompt in Prospero some paternal instinct, might inspire a tender attention to distract him from his labors, but he was nowhere to be found on the morning of Miranda's birth. When he did appear, he seemed to delight in the child's tiny fingers, her well-formed limbs, and yet his fascination lasted at most a month before strange habits again consumed him. While Bice raised Miranda, relishing her new role as a mother, Prospero's eccentricities and absences only increased.

His experiments had grown more frequent and more secretive. He disappeared now into his workrooms in the tunnels for weeks at a time, emerging only to demand the latest texts from Cairo and Baghdad, from Samarkand and Tiflis and the Far East. He employed a team of men in his service: grim, silent servants whose brutish looks frightened Agata as she passed them, guarding the entrances to the tunnels. These men left the castle on mysterious errands day and night, and the porter at the western gate told her of the covered carts they ferried in and out of the castle, the rumored midnight trips to the prisons and the foundling wheels along the canal. She did not understand what their work could be, but she knew the whole castle had begun to speak of it. She knew they wondered if their duke was of sound mind, and why, these past few years, Antonio had become the face of Milan, the de facto duke and representative of his noble family, while Prospero hid himself away.

She had urged Beatrice to intervene, and Bice had, to no avail. Agata heard her and Prospero screaming at each other in their rooms, only once, and then the fighting had ceased. Beatrice had become oddly tranquil, taking to her bed more frequently than she once had: she, who had always glowed with energy and health, with a robustness Agata could never match. She seemed to brighten whenever she and Agata left the castle together, when they went into the city or back to Franciacorta, and so Agata had begun taking her farther and farther from its walls, dreading the inevitable return to Prospero and his dark doings at the end of the day. This afternoon had been long and lovely, filled with Bice's laughter and Miranda's squeals. But the sun was quickly sinking, and Agata knew this day, like all those lovely others, would soon draw to an end.

"We should get back." Beatrice got to her feet, a touch unsteadily, still holding Miranda and the basket. "We should—" She took a step and stumbled, Miranda and the basket of apples tumbling to the ground.

"Bice," breathed Agata, and then she rushed to her side, pressing her hand to Bice's arm. "Bice! Bice, what's wrong?"

Her cousin's skin felt feverish to the touch, and she lay on the ground in a boneless heap, insensate to Miranda's keening cries. Never once had Bice ignored Miranda when she heard her crying. Never once had she abandoned her daughter, not in sickness, not in exhaustion, not in sadness.

Agata swept Miranda up and ran back to the waiting carriage, waving her arm to the driver, summoning him to help, *please help, come as quickly as you can.*

~

Bice's fever did not abate.

Prospero sent for the best doctors and healers he could find, caring not if their methods were medical or mystical. Agata seethed as charlatans spread unguents over Beatrice's skin, chanting in strange tongues as Bice lay unmoving under their hands. She attended Mass daily, begging God for Bice's recovery, begging him not to hold Bice accountable for her husband's sins.

Despite Agata's entreaties, Bice withered. Her strong limbs grew thin. Her face paled and sank in on itself. In the three weeks after that day in the hills she transformed, before Agata's eyes, into a living corpse. Three weeks, and Beatrice had pleaded with Agata, each of those endless days, to bring Miranda to her. She begged to let her see the daughter she could hear, down the hall, crying out for her mother, the mother who could not hold her, for fear that the illness plaguing Bice would infect her, too.

Miranda's screams reverberated throughout the castle for hours at a time, only strengthening in volume and frequency as the weeks dragged on. Agata grew to hate the child. The little beast wailed like a creature from Hell, and she beat her fists on Agata's chest whenever Agata attempted to hold her. She had everything of Prospero's temperament, and Agata could hardly help but abhor anything Prospero had made. She loathed herself for these thoughts, of course: she repented for them every morning in the pews, but she could not swallow the disdain she felt each time she laid her eyes upon Miranda's small, snotty face as she entered her room, the sense that

Miranda had taken from Bice something vital, something she needed now to live.

Agata did not bring Miranda to her mother. And so the halls were filled with their last yearning calls to each other, with Bice's moans and Miranda's sobs, in a castle otherwise as silent and still and patient as the tomb.

~

The day they buried Bice was cool and gray, and the clouds hung heavy with the threat of lightning. Agata stared at the tree above Prospero's head, the oak that loomed above Bice's graveside, and imagined it splitting. Imagined branches crashing down on Prospero's head, crushing him with their weight. Imagined his proud, ruined body laid to rest beneath the dirt, instead of Bice, beautiful, lost Bice, gone to live with the angels.

This was Agata's only solace: Bice was in Paradise now. Her soul was safe, her suffering finished. Christ had taken her into His embrace, and it was not for Agata to question why it had been so soon, so terribly soon, so cruelly, unbearably soon.

The last days of Bice's life had been the worst of them. She could not eat. She could not sleep. She twisted and writhed, and Agata struggled to pin down her arms so that she would not hurt herself, so that she would not scratch at her own eyes, as she had begun to do. "I see them," she would mutter, her voice raw and low. "I see them, and I know. Close my eyes, and I see them still. You can't make me sleep, Prospero. You can't make me—" These strange murmurings always ended in wracking spasms, and Agata stayed by Bice's side as she spat up blood, careful to keep it off her own skin. No one else had contracted Beatrice's illness. No one knew the cause. Agata thought of Bice's long months of lethargy and wondered if she should have known. Wondered if she should have taken Bice far from the castle, back to her parents' home and the lush vineyards she loved so well.

The day before she died, Bice had uttered words of blasphemy so profane that Agata struggled now to strike them from her memory. Bice's ravings were the words of a fever-addled mind. She didn't know what she was saying. But she had gripped Agata's hand, digging her ragged nails into the skin, beseeching her. Asking Agata to trespass against God, to commit a crime that would put both their souls in peril.

"Burn my body, Agata. Please, when I go. Burn it, and throw the ashes to the wind."

"No." Agata covered her mouth. "No, we would never cremate you, Bice. You don't know what you're saying."

"I beg of you, Agata, I beg—" She began a fit of coughing. "You must. There must be no trace of me. Take what remains to Franciacorta, and spread me in the hills. If I return, it will be as a tree, bearing fruit, living on through the wine. Agata—my sister—you must—"

Agata wrapped her fingers around Bice's wrist, bending low to speak into her ear. "You're delirious, Bice. You must rest. And you must not speak a word of this in the presence of the priests, or Archbishop d'Este will refuse to deliver your last rites." Already she and Antonio had struggled to convince the archbishop to set foot in the castle to attend to Bice, for the leaders of the Church detested Prospero. But they could hardly deny a dying woman her eternal reward simply because of the stories that swirled about her husband, as Antonio pointed out to them. There was no proof that Prospero's work and clandestine research violated the teachings of the Church. Perhaps he skirted the line at times, but Antonio could vouch for him as a brother, and he did, for Bice's sake. Prospero might be absent from Mass, but still, Antonio promised, he adhered to the will of God. His experiments were in God's service.

And so the black-frocked priests had come, and they had anointed Beatrice, and prayed over her, and delivered unto her the viaticum, though Beatrice had trouble getting the wafer past her lips. And in the end she passed away quietly, with no more talk of fire and smoke, with her eyes closed and Agata by her bedside. Prospero was absent for Beatrice's last breath, still whiling away at his false cures, still convinced he could save Bice, though the Lord above had granted her eternal rest.

Chapter 9

It was four days before Agata saw Bice again.

She walked through the portrait gallery for the first time since Bice's death and lingered before her cousin's portrait, the bright pinks and reds of its palette subdued by the waning midday light. The motionless, peaked woman in the frame looked more like Bice on her deathbed than when she was in full health. Bice was never that still. She was always in motion, always walking and laughing and talking, to everyone, to the cooks and the servants and the porters as easily as to the nobles she entertained at court. She asked them all to call her "Bice," even though Agata told her that she shouldn't.

With her passing, the castle had fallen under a black spell. Prospero was nowhere to be found: Agata knew of course that he had locked himself away in his workshops in the tunnels, but she dared not seek him out and demand that he present himself to his people in these days of mourning. She left that task to Antonio.

She left the portrait gallery and walked out to the courtyard. The storm that had loomed for days had never come, though the air still thrummed with dry, restless energy. A few servants crossed through the courtyard, all dressed in black. One of the young men, a dark-haired boy with a vulpine look about him, glanced up at her where she stood on the landing and detached himself from the entourage, gliding up the stairs.

He glanced around as he ascended the top step and then dropped his voice low. "Prospero requests your presence in the tunnels at midnight. He has something to show you."

She stared at him. "And he cannot tell me this himself? Who are you to tell me where I am to be and when?"

The boy shrugged. "Midnight, he says." He turned to go down the steps and then glanced back. "And he said not to tell his brother. Not yet."

She looked after the boy as he disappeared into the hall off the courtyard, the one where Virgil's statue stood guard.

~

Midnight came, and Agata found herself in the tunnels.

She had not intended to go. She had no desire to involve herself with Prospero's plans, whatever they might be. But she had tossed and turned in her bed an hour, and then she had gotten dressed, telling herself she would walk the halls to calm her nerves. She had walked, and walked. In the end her feet had carried her to one of the dark entrances to the labyrinth, the one near the armory, underneath which, she knew, Prospero's workrooms lay.

It was said the branching tunnels beneath Milan ran from the castle all the way to the countryside, though she had never gone that far. In fact Agata had never walked the tunnels on her own, but only with Bice, who was fascinated by them. "They're a feat of engineering, Agata! A perfect marriage of science and art. How can you help but explore all of this when it's right under you?"

Agata could help it easily. She wanted to return to the warmth of her bed, to await the comfort of dawn and the morning Mass she would attend. Yet she was curious why Prospero, who had never spoken to her alone, would request her presence in such cryptic fashion. So she traced the steps she remembered from her few trips with Bice, when Bice had showed her where Prospero did his mysterious work.

"This one makes little sparks," Bice had said, showing Agata a glass orb with metal inside, "and this one predicts the weather. And this is called an aludel, and this is an alembic, and—oh! In the next room he stores his athanor. Isn't it a wonderful word, 'athanor'? Let's go see." It was clear Beatrice knew how to work the strange contraptions, and Agata had to hold herself back from telling

Bice, once again, that such instruments were surely sinful; the harsh way their foreign names scraped at the ear made that clear enough. Bice had never listened, and afterwards she would barely speak to Agata for days. Agata could never bear Beatrice's silence for long.

That was long ago, when Prospero still let Bice enter his rooms freely.

Agata sighed and pressed on into the darkness, torch in hand. She hesitated before the great iron door of Prospero's laboratorium, unsure if her decision to come had been wise. But before she could turn back, the door swung open, and Prospero ushered her in with the sweep of his massive arm. "Midnight is the time of miracles, Agata. And this night is filled with them. Come inside and see what I have made."

She crept into the room, a shiver running down her spine as Prospero closed the heavy door behind her. He crossed to the opposite side, to the apogee of the half circle in which they stood, and thrust open the door there, summoning her with a crook of the finger. "Follow me, Agata. Follow, and fear not."

She knew the room they entered contained books upon books: she had seen it before, with Bice. What she did not expect, however, was for Prospero to run his hand down the side of one of the many bookshelves, the one just across from the doorway, and for the bookshelf to move. It swung back to reveal yet another entrance, this one unlit, a dark cavern concealed behind Prospero's multitudinous tomes.

Prospero vanished into the darkness, and Agata followed, as if in a trance. She saw now the true design of Prospero's lair. The workrooms she had seen with Bice were only the first level of the laboratorium. Set around them, behind them, were other rooms, and around those a tunnel, the narrow tunnel she and Prospero were walking through. They turned to the right, though she saw that it also continued on to the left, meaning it must ring the full crescent of his workspace. From this tunnel, one could enter any of the hidden rooms through the closed doors they were passing. They passed one, then two, and then came to a third, to the very end of the passage.

Prospero stopped and turned to face her, the light from her torch flickering over the ridges and dips of his broad face.

"You will see wonders untold tonight, Agata. Your mind may not at first comprehend them, but remember that your own Bible is full of tales of such marvels, such feats of grace. Remember that Jesus of Nazareth rose after three days, and Lazarus four. Remember the words with which the apostle Paul urged us to empty Sheol and rob death of its ill-begotten prize. 'I will ransom them from the power of the grave; I will redeem them from death:

O death, I will be thy plagues; O grave, I will be thy destruction.'"

Never before had Prospero quoted Scripture in Agata's presence, or, in fact, indicated that he had any knowledge of its teachings. He meant to enthrall her, to beguile her in some way. Her heart beat fast in her chest, for she feared she grasped some meaning in the muddled message of his semi-blasphemous ramblings. "Prospero," she managed, her throat choked, "what is behind this door? What have you done?"

He pressed a large hand against the door and opened it. Agata could see nothing at first. Only a dim light, playing off the wall. Prospero urged her forward, and she came to stand before him, staring into the cell he had revealed.

A figure sat in the center of its confines. It wore a shroud, and its shoulders were hunched, as if it might at any moment keel over. Agata breathed in, trying to calm the hammering in her chest. "Prospero—"

"She was never lost, Agata." He passed by Agata and stepped into the cell, filling it with his mass. "Never gone." He pulled off the figure's veil, holding it high as he crumpled it in his fist. "She has been returned to us, by the great powers of this universe, wielded through my hands."

Agata staggered back, her hand flying to her mouth.

It was Bice.

Some infernal copy of Bice. Bice as though she had been a thousand years at the bottom of the sea, her skin washed to a stony blue-green, her lips the blanched color of dead coral, her hair as lank and tangled as kelp.

The thing peered at Agata, its eyes focusing with great difficulty, and stretched out a skeletal hand. "Gata," it rasped, from somewhere deep in its ruined throat. "Gata."

"What have you done?" Agata's voice was low, but it seemed to boom in the small stone space. Prospero looked at her, a smirk on his lips.

"I have returned her to this mortal plane, of course, from which she was expelled so cruelly. I have rescued her from Purgatory, Agata. The corrupt Church claims its priests, fattened with cheese and wine they've bought off the backs of peasants, can hasten one's entrance into Heaven. Why can the journey not work the other way? For those who were taken too soon, who have so many more years to live: Why should we not return them to Earth, to their rightful home, if we have the power, if we have the will?"

"Sacrilege," Agata gasped. The thing's eyes were still on her, and she could hardly bear its stare.

"No." Prospero drew himself up to his full height. "I have consulted with the true masters of the Church. I have received their blessing for my efforts. Not all will agree, of course, but I have the support of many. The ones who see reason are on my side."

Lies, thought Agata, but this time she did not speak aloud. She kept her eye on the creature, which reached for her still. Could it be some copy? Some phantasm, meant to deceive? But she knew Bice's face better than her own. She knew Bice's every expression. And the look etched into each line of this being's hauntingly familiar face was terror.

She had seen that look not very long ago. She had seen it as Beatrice begged Agata to burn her body and scatter the ashes to the wind.

"Had her soul gone on to Heaven, to its final resting place, I never could have retrieved it. She was in Purgatory, for she was never meant to be taken from us so soon. But I have restored that spark of life unjustly plundered from her form by completing the great and difficult work of anastasis. It was a noble art once known to Christian mages in the Holy Land, though the knowledge was lost over centuries. I have reconstructed their writings, and now, once again, we hold the ability to create life where there was only death, to turn back the mindless tides of fate."

Agata knew Prospero's tricks. She knew his powers of persuasion. His effort to exert them upon her, to convince her this was some pious and necessary act, stunk of deception. But she did not care. Here was Bice. Her Bice, Bice pulled from the safety of her grave bed. And she looked so very scared.

She came forward, taking Bice's cold, waxy hand with only the slightest flinch. "It's all right," she murmured, trying not to breathe too deeply of the fetid scent rising from her cousin's skin. "It will be all right."

Prospero relaxed, stepping back. "You see, Agata? She needs someone to care for her. I must attend to other pressing matters and cannot be with her always. The world does not stop turning, even for wonders such as this." He looked down at her, his eyes black voids in the torchlight. "Will you help her and not say a word to Antonio? He will not understand, not yet. We must give her time, time to recover, and then present her to him when she is truly whole again."

She felt a pang, thinking how Antonio would rejoice to see Bice's face again, though his horror would surely match her own. "Yes." Her voice was but a whisper. "I will help her. Tell me what she needs."

~

She spent the first night washing the filth from Bice's limbs, tending to the body she had seen expire only days before. The body that even now should be sleeping beneath the dirt, its soul gone to claim its eternal reward.

Agata bathed Bice's body in a ceramic tub Prospero had set in the room beside his blazing alchemical furnace, where the air was a little warmer, though she did not know that Bice could feel it. "Too much liquid on the skin will cause deterioration," Prospero warned. "Use sparingly this rosewater, which ameliorates the smell." He delivered his instructions the way he used to dictate certain household tasks, as if bathing a corpse were in no way extraordinary. Perhaps, Agata reflected, it was not for him. She had heard the stories about the foundling wheels and prisons. If his claims were true, unbaptized infants and criminals were perfect candidates for his form of redemption from Limbo and Purgatory alike. How many unfortunates had he brought back before Bice? How long did they last? How long did Bice have?

Bice looked at her with dull, glaucous eyes as Agata ran a cloth lightly over her arm. She had bits of grime stuck to her in all kinds of places, but Agata dared not scrub the patches too hard. She did not know what was part of Bice's body now. Even if Prospero had halted her decay, rot had set in the moment she drew her last natural breath.

"Gata," the creature said again, and Agata closed her eyes. Bice knew her, but Agata could not tell if she knew anything else. Did she understand what Prospero had done? Did she think? Was she truly Bice, or only a shell? In either case, Agata knew she would keep her promise not to tell Antonio, however unwillingly. Bice's soul was in peril, caught here in this liminal state, and she did not know what would become of Bice's spirit if harm befell this body. She had to tread carefully. Prospero believed that she trusted him, that she credited his miracle. She would keep him believing until she could determine what to do.

The creature muttered something else. Agata ignored Bice's complaint, patting her arm dry, until the word came again, this time clearer, more insistent.

"Mranda." A kind of grunt, all running together. "Mranda. Mranda."

Agata dropped the cloth, staring at Bice's face. Bice turned slightly to fix her gaze upon Agata, moving her lips more deliberately now, the motion slow but certain. "Mi . . . ran . . . da. Mir . . . anda. Miranda."

"Bice—"

"Miranda."

"Bice—" The world spun. Agata had performed this exchange over and over in the days before Bice's passing, but death had not stopped Bice's moans. Even now, she was crying out for her daughter. Even now, with this impossible animation, with her mind rotted by death, Miranda was all she wanted.

Chapter 10

Over the next few weeks, Agata spent the daylight hours in a daze and the long nights by Bice's side in the subterranean warren that had become her home.

Now that he felt he had won her loyalty, Prospero hardly deigned to address Agata at all, unless he had some new instruction in her care of Bice. He did not allow her to enter his other rooms, though she could hear muffled thuds and groans from them many of the nights that she visited and feel the occasional shaking of the walls. At those times she held Bice's hand tightly, for Bice trembled whenever she heard these sounds, and Agata wondered, as she had so many times, what Bice had gone through to return to this body, to this realm.

They stayed together in Bice's cell, which Agata had endeavored to make feel a bit more like Bice's grand bedroom in the ducal apartments. She brought down blankets, and tapestries to hang on the walls, and a few of Bice's things: her favorite rings, her lyre, her little collection of books. Bice had always devoured anything that she could read, from the family Bible to the impenetrable mathematical texts Prospero allowed her to borrow because it amused him. Now, however, she only held the books in her hands, as if they were objects whose purpose she could not recall. Never once did Agata see her open them to a page.

Just as she fixed up Bice's quarters, so too did Agata attempt to improve Bice herself. She rouged her cheeks, and colored her lips, and dressed Bice in some of her old gowns. It always felt as though she were dressing Bice for her funeral anew. After all her fussing, Bice looked more human: still nothing like the vibrant and irrepressible woman she had been in the full bloom of her health, but Agata knew that woman was gone. What remained was a revenant. And yet every night she spent with Bice threw Agata into confusion, distancing her from the castle staff, still caught up in their mourning, still lamenting the loss of their duchess.

Prospero had of course revealed this particular secret to no one else, though she discovered, from her nights in the cells, that he had his own trusted forces inside the castle. She saw the slender servant boy who had summoned her to the workrooms that fateful night pass in and out of the laboratorium. A dozen others she knew, others she'd seen in sunlight. They acknowledged one another with nods, and she knew they would never speak of this in the world above. If they had made some pact with Prospero, she would not reveal them to Antonio. After all, she had made her own.

She had tried to seek answers from different priests in confession, revealing nothing of her true identity. But when she began to speak of souls brought back into dead bodies, they either dismissed her outright or reacted with vitriol, telling her she must never speak of such dark and vile sins. "These awful imaginings corrupt the virtuous, especially in the female mind, which is swayed and seduced far more easily than the male," Father Rossi of Santa Maria delle Grazie told her. "Recite thrice the Hail Mary. Reflect upon the purity of our most beloved mother and banish such wicked thoughts from your mind."

It brought Agata no peace to think about mothers these days. She did not wish to dwell upon the strength and serenity that motherhood brought, for Bice still considered herself a mother and knew her child was only floors away. She asked for Miranda incessantly, picking up new phrases as the days dragged on. "Bring me . . . Miranda." "I want . . . Miranda." "Please . . . I need . . . to see . . . Miranda."

Agata did not know if it was due to the fumes that pervaded Prospero's workrooms or her own true feeling for her cousin's plight, but she had begun to consider the idea. Miranda would not necessarily know there was anything wrong with her mother, so glad would she be to see her again. And if she spoke of what she saw in the tunnels, it would only be the babblings of a child, a child who had made the servants' lives a hell these past few weeks. She threw ceaseless tantrums, thrusting herself at the wall, digging her nails into the exposed flesh of anyone who came near her, urinating on the floor though she was old enough to know better. Agata had never seen the like. The child was too small to beat properly, in the manner Agata felt would improve her behavior. Only Prospero could subdue her, when he came to the nursery to comfort her, which he hardly did enough.

After one of these daylong crying jags from Miranda, and after descending to the tunnels to find Bice making the same plaintive request she always made, Agata confronted Prospero. He was working in one of his inner rooms, but she hammered on the door until he opened it, attempting to stand strong under his withering gaze.

"We should bring her Miranda," she began, pushing out the words in a rush. "Their cleaving has left them both inconsolable, and nothing else will heal this rift. Let me bring Miranda here for only an hour, maybe two. Every fifth night, let's say, so that they have something to look forward to."

Prospero looked down at her with the distant expression he often wore, as though he were God Himself and she some unworthy petitioner, begging for His mercy. "No."

"No?" She felt her cheeks flush at his refusal. "Your Grace, if they continue on this way, both of them will lose their minds. You cannot give a mother life again and keep her from her child!"

"I can." He started to close the door, but Agata stuck a foot into the doorway. She breathed hard for a moment as he studied her, afraid that he might strike. But he only laughed. "One day, perhaps, Agata. One day, when the world I wish to make is manifest. This age has little room for genius, for vision. But it will change. I promise you; it will change."

He pushed her back gently and closed the door.

∼

The next night Agata almost abstained from visiting the tunnels. Prospero was away for the first time since Bice's resurrection, on a trip to Turin, the purpose of which he had shared with no one. Agata doubted piety had anything to do with the pilgrimage. He had instructed Agata to care for Bice in his absence, but he would not know if she failed to visit. It pained Agata to see Bice night after night, pained her to touch this living ghost of her cousin, to try to comfort her, while having no idea what to do to help her or who she might turn to for aid in undoing Prospero's evil work. But in the end she could not bear the thought of Bice sobbing her dry tears through the night, expecting Agata to come. And so she went, the key to the workrooms in hand, since Prospero would not be there to let her in.

She was surprised to find Beatrice out of her cell when she came into the laboratorium but was glad to see Prospero had let her wander a little. When Agata entered, Bice was in the room with all the books, sitting on the stone floor with no regard for its chill and leafing through the pages with her long, pale fingers. Agata saw illustrations of monsters and flayed-open bodies in the volume Beatrice held and averted her eyes, unwilling to so much as look upon the manuals for Prospero's black magic. "Put those away, Bice. These books are unholy, and every one should be burned."

Bice looked up at her with milky-blue eyes. "I'm ... learning."

She sounded for a moment like her old self, which somehow hurt Agata more than anything else had. Agata snatched up the foul book. "Read the texts I brought you, Beatrice. No good can come from these." She replaced the book in its space on the shelf and offered her hand to Bice, who took it, standing unsteadily.

They sat together for hours that night, free of Prospero's presence, and Agata read Beatrice passages from the Book of Psalms by candlelight. Only later—much later—did she realize Bice had not asked for Miranda once.

~

Agata awoke to screaming.

It had been her custom to return to her bed for two or three hours before the sun rose, to get some sleep before the rest of the castle began its day in earnest. She felt that she had barely been in bed a half hour before she heard the commotion coming from the direction of Miranda's room, just a few doors down from her own.

She shook off sleep and wrapped her shawl around her shoulders, stepping out into the cold hallway. The shrieking was farther off now, as if someone were moving through the courtyard. She listened to the repetitive sound, her mind too sluggish to perceive it as anything more than a bird cry. But then a word began to take shape, and her feet moved almost before her brain had grasped the meaning. *"Bice! Bice! Biiiiiceeeee!"*

She ran. She ran, fire and darkness blurring around her. She ran and she ran and she nearly tumbled down the stairs, following the screams. There were more of them now. Many more, a chorus, spreading through the walls.

She skidded to a stop as she came to the kitchens, for she could no longer determine the source of the sirens. The wall of sound pushed her to her knees, shaking with the knowledge of what must have transpired, what the name she heard all around her must mean.

Bice had escaped. Had Agata locked the rooms as she left them? She remembered the press of the gold key in her hand, the burn of her muscles as she pulled shut the solid iron door, but the hour was late, and she was exhausted, bone-weary after weeks of shock and strangeness. Had she left the door open so that Bice could leave? Had she meant to free her, somewhere deep inside of her mind, somewhere that could not deny Bice the right to see her child?

It seemed impossible. And yet: she could not be sure.

"Agata." The sound of her name cut through the clamor, though spoken at a volume much lower. Antonio staggered towards her, his sword drawn, his eyes wild. "Agata, it's Bice. She—Prospero has—"

"I know." She could not deny it. She stayed kneeling before him, and the words came out as a plea for mercy. "I know, Antonio."

He stared down at her for a long moment and then seized her by the elbow, pulling her to her feet. "You aided him."

"I did not. I only—"

"You *conspired*"—he jabbed a shaking finger into her chest—"you cavorted with forces of darkness, you perverted her memory, the memory of sweet Beatrice, who should have died ere wicked Prospero could make her his bride. Better *you* had died ere you beshrewed her—"

She slapped him, the smack ringing out above the cries. He raised high his sword and then grabbed her wrist, dragging her to a cell in the northern tower.

~

It took a long time for Agata to reconstruct all that unfolded in the days that followed.

Scraps of stories were passed to her between the bars of her cell by the servant women, along with her meager meals. Patrizia, long the person Agata could count on to tell her when anything of vital note occurred in the servants' quarters, informed her that Stella, Miranda's night nurse, had awoken to see a figure standing over Miranda's bed, lifting the girl into its arms. Stella had screamed, and then the figure had come towards her, its finger laid over its lips. She saw, though she could hardly believe it, that the phantom wore the face of the duchess Beatrice.

They had struggled over the child for a few moments until Stella's howling brought the guards from the entrance of the ducal apartments, who froze in place when they saw who held the duke's daughter in her arms. Bice darted past them, running down the halls, and they gave chase, following Bice to the tunnels and finally wresting the child from her grasp when she tripped, falling to the ground.

"And then?" Agata shuddered to think what might have happened to Bice after her capture. "What did they do to her then?"

Patrizia lifted her hands, palms up. "Nothing. They were afraid to touch her, and let her go. Antonio was livid. No one has been able to find her, though Antonio has guards combing every inch of the tunnels."

Agata hated the flare of hope that thrilled her heart. She should not want Bice to escape. She should want this awful saga to come to an end. But the Beatrice she had once known would have run and found the best hiding spot she could. Antonio's men could search those unmapped tunnels a thousand years and not find Bice if she wanted not to be found.

But Agata knew Beatrice would not last long. Prospero's magic was not perfected: he himself had told her as much. Whatever animated Bice's bones would fade soon, and she would die anew down there, perishing in the lonely maze like a rat. *Let her soul be saved,* Agata pleaded as she waited in her cell, to the God she was no longer certain heeded her tainted prayers. *Grant her entrance into your kingdom, O Lord, once her long suffering is done.*

Patrizia reported that Miranda was under armed guard day and night, and that Prospero had not yet returned from Turin. Agata knew this last part, for Antonio had told her what awaited him when he did. He had come to her cell the day after Bice's escape and demanded she give over the identities of all Prospero's lackeys and the keys to his rooms. She had done it. She had told him again that she had not taken part in Prospero's dark deeds but only tried to ensure the salvation of Bice's soul. "Tell that to the gulls," he told her, his voice as sharp as a knife, "when we send you out to sea with my villainous brother. You have cast your lot with him. God, and Milan, will judge you both for his crimes."

She trembled as he left her, but she did not cry. She had no tears left to shed. She only hoped that Prospero's spies would alert him to the coup brewing within the castle walls, and that he would stay away, far away, so that she never had to see his face again. She could think of no worser fate than facing her sentence by Prospero's side.

She would sooner take her own life, though the sin was mortal. If they pushed a barge with both her and Prospero into the sea, she would jump from it and swim until her limbs gave out, swim until she sank.

~

Prospero did return. He returned for Miranda and damned her by so doing.

Antonio delivered the news to Agata himself, the day before he freed her from the cells. "They say the false duke returns this evening. The king of Naples has men at the ready to back me when he does. The priests have come to me to plead your case and beg me to allow the salvation of your soul. On their word alone I will liberate you, once Prospero and the girl are gone. But know that no penance will satisfy me, Agata." He leaned closer to the bars, and she could smell his musk, as though he were the trapped animal, not she. "You live by my largess, but forgiveness I will never grant."

She let the emotion drain out of her. She had loved this man, but she would not love again. If love had made Prospero do what he did, she wanted no part of it. She only wanted quiet now. She only wanted peace. "I understand," she said dully. And then her mind snagged on the other part he had just said, the part fear and hunger had caused her to skip over. "The girl . . . Miranda? You're sending Miranda to die?"

"Better that she perish before she learns what a monster her father is. What a monster he made of her mother. Better that she die than become a monster herself."

"You can't mean that."

"Do you believe any child born to a man like that

could escape his influence, Agata? Do you? Bice could not save him, could not change him, and if not for him she would have taken her place among the saints. Any child of his seed will bloom as poisoned fruit, whether he is here or not."

Agata heard the truth in his words. Prospero's corruption had already crept into Miranda's character, she was certain of it. But Bice's heart would break, wherever she was, if she ever learned of her daughter's fate. "Let me keep the child, please. Let me raise her. Let me save her."

Antonio let out a barking laugh. "You? You, preserve her from evil? I would rather she be reared by a common bitch than fall into your clutches, woman. No, the child cannot live. Prospero's line will end, and his reign will be nothing more than distant memory."

"If you let them leave, she will be his. He will smother every spark of goodness in her. She will become a demon, Antonio, raised without faith, without hope of redemption."

"She will never live that long. The seas are stormy, and God in His wrath will destroy them, for Prospero has committed the ultimate transgression against Him and the order of His world. Let the sea take them and scatter their bones. Let the fish feast on their flesh, and let the name Prospero never be heard again in all of fair Milan."

~

From that day forward, as Antonio decreed, Prospero's name was seldom heard. But Bice's name still echoed through the halls. Only out of Antonio's hearing; only as a story. A ghostly tale, passed on in whispers. Agata knew that young men and women sneaked away from court dances to look upon the portrait in the gallery and to try to find the place in the tunnels where Bice had lived. She chased them off whenever she found them lurking near the painting, and the workrooms were locked, their contents turned over to Naples as evidence in Prospero's hasty midnight trial. Agata heard the court there did not believe the fantastical tales of the old duke's wife come back to life. King Alonso hardly cared as long as Milan bent the knee.

Antonio had ordered Prospero's portrait moved to the family vaults, perhaps fearing some supernatural retribution for its destruction, but had left Bice's portrait alone, save for the shroud he commanded the servants to hang over its frame, the shroud he forbid them to lift. He himself lifted it, though. Agata knew, for she had come upon him there, standing in the galleries, and she had let him be, let him look upon Beatrice's countenance for as long as he liked, though she herself could not bear the sight. She welcomed the covering, for it felt like the only true burial Beatrice had been granted.

She held her own funeral for Bice and Miranda, though there were no bodies. She went to the plot where Beatrice's body once lay, and placed some of their garments beneath the dirt, and prayed for hours under the shade of the towering oak. She thought about leaving Milan, once the deed was done, but she had nowhere else to go. She seldom returned to Franciacorta. Her aunt and uncle seemed to blame her for Bice's death, as though she had failed, in some way, to protect their only child. Their faces were drawn and wan, and they both, it transpired, did not have long left to live. She went home for the respective funerals and never ventured back again.

A year later, Antonio finally married, choosing as his bride the fair Isabella della Torre, who died not two years later in childbirth. Their son did not survive, as Agata remembered well. And yet she could see the child's face; and yet she could imagine his laugh, the way he would run around the castle, pulling at skirts and pleading for treats. There had been no little boy, no little duke with Antonio's dark eyes and his mother's auburn hair. Antonio had never taken him to Africa, on his very first trip abroad, to see the marriage of the princess of Naples to the king of Tunis. Whatever she remembered was only a wishful dream.

~

Agata's days passed a dozen years in drudgery. Antonio ignored or abused her at his leisure. The servant girls seemed to grow younger as she grew older, and stupider by the year. Patrizia had long since passed away in the last plague. All her friends were gone from this world. She was thirty-three years old, and she longed for this lingering life to pass. Daily Mass was her only peace.

She preferred the Duomo to the closer-by Santa Maria delle Grazie and to the smaller castle chapel Antonio had revived after many years of disuse under Prospero's reign. The Duomo, with its sky-reaching ceilings and perpetual construction, reminded her that the work of God on earth was still unfinished. The kingdom of Heaven, in its perfection, was not yet revealed to man. Stone by stone, they would create it here.

As she walked back one Sunday with a contingent from the castle, she saw as they approached the gates that a caravan was passing through. Perhaps Antonio had returned from his trip to Tunis, for he had been due to stay a few days afterward in Naples.

She came through the gates and entered the courtyard to find servants running hither and thither, talking amongst themselves in murmurs. She took hold of one girl's arm as she passed, arresting her mid-step. "What's going on here? Has Duke Antonio returned?"

The girl looked at her with wide eyes. "Antonio is the duke no longer. Haven't you heard? The old duke is returned. And his daughter—" She pointed towards the landing, where a dark-haired young woman stood. "His daughter—"

At the sight of the woman's face, Agata's heart nearly stopped. Bice had returned. Bice had left the tunnels, had survived this decade and more. Bice—

Miranda—

Bice—

Miranda!

Bile rose in her throat as she realized the truth, as she took in the girl's meaning. The old duke is returned. "Get her something to cover her face," she hissed to the girl. "Do not allow her to take it off. Tell the rest—if they permit her to so much as lift it for a moment, they will answer to me." The girl gaped at her, and Agata thrust her away. "Go! Now!"

The girl fled, and Agata walked in the opposite direction as fast as she could, seeking refuge in the halls. She walked, and she gasped, and her hands began to tremble, and she feared that she would faint, when she turned a corner and there—

He's here.

There—

He sees us!

There was the old duke, the Devil himself, his eyes as blue as the sea meant to drown him. "Hello, Miranda," he said, but that was wrong. She wasn't Miranda, she was—

He knows we aren't Agata, Dorothea, he knows—

"Playing games?" He came towards her, one slow step at a time. "Messing about in minds? Leave the magic to me, girl. You meddle in what you do not understand."

It's only a dream. Miranda felt the terror shooting through her, the blood pumping and the throat tightening back in the body she had forgotten she had. *A dream, a dream, a dream—*

He was closing in. Miranda could feel Dorothea nowhere. *We have to get back. We have to get out. He sees me, he sees—*

Her father held out his hand. "Let me help you. You've wandered off the path and into dark woods, Miranda. Let me help you sleep."

Agata-Miranda recoiled and forced herself to remember Dorothea's smile. Her touch, her laugh, her presence in the real world, the world beyond this shadow play. Somewhere out there, Dorothea lay beside her, and Miranda needed to find her.

"Miranda—"

She could hear it. There. Below his voice. Below the sounds of the castle, the vivid illusions of this recent past.

A pounding, even and steady. Two rhythms, entwined. Her pulse, and Dorothea's, beating fingertip to fingertip.

The world began to dissolve around her. She saw her father snatching at the air as she sank into blackness, swallowed by the void. Around her she heard laughter. Howling, hysterical laughter, not Ariel's voice, but a thousand screeching wails, a cacophony, tearing at her eardrums. They drowned out the twin pulses, and she grasped for purchase against the slippery sides of the void. *Dorothea!* she cried out. Then, in the voice of the child she had once been, she pleaded now as she had pleaded then: *Mother! Mother! Mother!*

Chapter 11

Miranda tumbled back into herself, panting, staring at the angels on the ceiling, the bed beneath her firm, the world around her real.

"We made it." Her voice did not sound like her own, so long had she been in Agata's mind. "We made it. Dorothea, we—"

She stopped, for Dorothea's hand was not in hers. She turned and saw that Dorothea's lips were blue. A dark stream of blood dribbled from her nose.

"No," Miranda breathed. She forced herself up, against her body's protest, and leaned over Dorothea, cupping her face in her hands. "Dorothea, please. We made it. We're alive. You have to wake up. Please."

I've never known anyone whose brother and sister died before. I've never known anyone who died before.

"Dorothea, you *have* to." Miranda's voice cracked, and she pressed frantic kisses to Dorothea's lips, her cheeks, her closed, unmoving eyelids. "Duriya. Dorothea, come back to me. Come back to me, please! I love you, Dorothea, I love—"

Dorothea's chest heaved, and she burst into a flurry of violent coughing.

Miranda gripped her shoulders as Dorothea convulsed, nearly falling from the bed. "In my pouch—" Dorothea gasped. "The mithridate—"

Miranda bolted across the room, grabbing the pouch and fumbling for the small stoppered alabastrum left inside. She ran back to Dorothea, who took hold of the container of mithridate and swallowed it in one draught, though she gagged and coughed as she forced the substance down. She quieted, staying still for a long moment as Miranda stroked her back, and then looked up at Miranda with bloodshot eyes.

"He . . ."

"I know." Miranda's mind was still filled with visions of what her father had done. The sight, the smell of it. The feel of her mother's hand, cold and heavy in Agata's palm. "Did he really see us? There, at the end—was it him?"

Dorothea shook her head. "I don't think so. I can't see any reason he would be walking in Agata's dreams, Miranda. He couldn't have known we would go there. I think it may have been our own fear, or the demons of the void, toying with us. I could hear them, there, at the end. I—" She shuddered, looking down at her arm, as though she bore scratches there. "I felt them."

"Me too."

They both fell silent. Dorothea got out of the bed, swaying slightly on her feet. "I should leave. You should go to Naples, Miranda. To Ferdinand." She started towards the portal leading to the tunnels. "He can protect you."

"Wait! Don't go." Miranda followed her, taking hold of her elbow and guiding her back to sit on the edge of the bed. "Dorothea, stop, please. I do not know what the future brings, it's true, nor where we go from here. But I do know that I want you there with me." She softened her tone, lest the words sound like a command. "If you want to be, I mean."

Dorothea did not speak for a long moment, and Miranda thought she would refuse her. "I do want to be," she finally said, her voice raw. "But even if we discard your royal titles when we're alone—even if we pretend you're not to be Ferdinand's queen—I don't want to be your servant, Miranda. I know that's how I entered your life, but I can't bear the thought of continuing on that way. It's hard enough for me to imagine finding happiness as your mistress, much less your maid. I can't promise you anything now. Let's survive this madness, and then we'll speak of what might be."

Miranda clasped her hand. "Of course. I'm sorry. I never should have let you clean these rooms, never sat and watched while you toiled. I wouldn't now. It's only that—" She sighed. "On my island, it was different. My father bid spirits to do our work, and forced Caliban into labor, telling me all the time it was the natural order of things. It's taken me a long time to understand life here. But that's no excuse. I should have let you know how I feel about you, Dorothea. I'm sorry that I didn't, until I thought I'd lost you."

Dorothea smiled at her weakly. "So you'll scrub the floors and dust the shelves in Naples? You, on your noble knees?"

Miranda laughed. "And more." She sombered. "But I fear that neither Ferdinand nor King Alonso can aid us. You saw what my father can do, Dorothea. Even death will not deter him. He will come after me, wherever I go."

"He was defeated once, Miranda. He can be stopped again."

"His power is far greater now. You didn't see him on the island. I didn't understand it then, but now I do. He was refining his magic. Perfecting his art. I believe he could turn this whole city to ash, Dorothea. He could make all of Italy bow to him and do his bidding. Antonio is right. He could rule the world." She shivered. "He must need more time for his plans, though, or he would have already made his move. We must act quickly."

"What do we do?"

"You remember the figure that brought me to the galleries during the ball? The one wearing the mask?"

"Yes, of course."

"I think—Dorothea, it seems impossible, but I think that may have been my mother."

Dorothea's eyes grew wide. "After all these years? How would her body have endured?"

"I don't know. Perhaps she found someone to help her, or discovered a kind of magic to preserve herself. She loved to learn." Miranda's throat tightened on this last word. Now that she was back in her own form, she could fully feel the pain of seeing her mother, her lovely, laughing, living mother, and losing her once more. "Antonio doesn't appear to have left his cell in all the days of his confinement. I don't think it was him. It was her."

"So she wanted you to find out. She wanted you to see her portrait."

"Yes, I think so. She'll help us, Dorothea, if she's still within these walls. We should go to the tunnels. See if we can find any trace of her. Together we can free my uncle, and all of us—you, me, Antonio—will go to Naples and warn Ferdinand of what's coming." She tightened her grip on Dorothea's hand. "Is there a spell you can do that would reveal her to us? Some way we could find her, if she walks the world still?"

Dorothea blew out a long breath. "That kind of magic is far beyond my skill. Prospero plunges into the sort of dark pools in which other mages wouldn't dare dabble. I wouldn't even know where to look for details of such rituals, or who to ask."

So their magic was no match for her father's. And on their side they had no firm allies: only the ghost of her mother, which might be nothing more than Miranda's own fancy, and her treacherous uncle, who might murder Miranda as soon as come to her aid. "We've no choice, then. We'll search the tunnels tomorrow and see if we can find a way to release Antonio. We need someone King Alonso will believe, when we come to his court. But we must watch our backs with him, Dorothea. I'm still Prospero's daughter. You heard the way he talked about me."

"I know." Dorothea raised her hand to run the fingers along Miranda's cheekbone. "But don't listen to your uncle and Agata, eh? That was long ago. They didn't know you then, and they don't know you now. You're nothing like him, Miranda. I promise you."

Miranda brought Dorothea's hand to her lips, brushing a kiss over the knuckles. "Whatever we do come morrow, we both need to sleep. I'll help clean you up, and then you should rest. We still have hours until the dawn."

Dorothea did not fight her. She acquiesced to Miranda's ministrations, and they fell asleep together, a fitful sleep, laced with shared and terrible visions that were not their own.

~

In the last hours before morning, Miranda dreamed of a paradise.

All around her a lush jungle stretched out, as far as the eye could see. In the distance, she could hear the calling waves.

It was like her island, but far vaster. A world of wonder, with sickness banished, with death long gone. In her ears echoed the lilting songs of birds she loved, their flocks hale and huge, swooping high in the shade, darting in and out of the canopy. Creatures ran around her feet, rabbits and lizards and frogs, uncrushed by man, untormented by larger beasts, living in eternal idyll. Above her, the sky was endless and blue, a shade almost purpureal, cushioning flocculent clouds in its fathomless depths.

She heard someone calling. The voice of someone she loved. Everyone she loved was here, forever. Everyone she loved was safe, at last. She knew what it was to love, at last. This was a perfect world, the world she had never even known she wanted. This was Heaven, brought down to earth, and tears streamed down her cheeks as she beheld its infinite perfection. She never wanted to leave this place. She wished to stay, and knew she could not: not yet. *Not yet. Not yet, Miranda. Not yet.*

She awoke, crying, to find Dorothea gone.

~

The rain came heavy that morning, and its damp cold traveled through the floor up Miranda's limbs, chilling her to the bone.

Dorothea had slipped away to avoid being caught, Miranda was sure of it. But still she worried, and still she paced the floor. Her head ached with all that she had experienced, and nausea overtook her in waves, the potion from the night before leaving her shaky and sick. She hoped Dorothea was faring better. She had meant what she said, that she wanted Dorothea by her side, always: But what bargain had she offered her? Did she mean for Dorothea to be her mistress? Was that a life for either of them?

The sentiment, so clear in her fear of losing Dorothea to the void, began to congeal into something murkier. Perhaps it was selfish to even present the choice to Dorothea, to offer this half life. Perhaps it was naive, for surely Ferdinand would not leave her to her own devices as she had so often been left alone here. She would be expected to join the court and manage the household, and surely he would want children. She understood now, from being in Agata's head, how important that was, the bearing of an heir. She understood so much more now. She understood what her life in Naples was to be, what the life of a woman within castle walls looked like. It was the life she had been born to, but maybe Dorothea could find a better one. Maybe Miranda could help her, even if it meant Dorothea would leave Miranda behind.

She looked out the window at the water pouring down the panes, pushing such thoughts aside. They had to survive this trial first, as Dorothea had said. Then they could think of the future. If they could escape her father, perhaps—perhaps—they could find happiness, even if they could not find it together. King Alonso would welcome them, she was certain of it. He had only brought her father home because he needed Prospero to calm the seas for the fleet's return to Italy, but it was Milan's tribute he wanted, and Antonio he trusted to give it to him. She liked Antonio not, but he had ruled in peace. He had managed the state well and kept his people from sickness and starvation. He was nothing like her father. She understood all this from Agata, too. If she backed Antonio's claim, her marriage to Ferdinand would count towards his alliance with Naples. But if Naples could not save her from Prospero, she had nowhere else to turn.

The doorknob to her bedroom turned, and she spun, hoping Dorothea had been sent. Instead she looked upon Agata's face, and she found herself grinning. "Agata!" She got to her feet. "It's good to see you. May I help you with that tray?"

Agata glared at her. "Sit down." She crossed to the table, Miranda's breakfast teetering upon the tray she held. Miranda obeyed her, unable to tear her eyes from Agata's face. How strange, to look from the outside at eyes she had peered out of, only hours before. She knew now the worlds within Agata, the depths. She had felt Agata's distaste for her; but she understood that, too. Agata had been frightened for Bice's sake. She had hated Prospero, and everything he made, because she loved Beatrice so. Miranda could understand that. Perhaps she could tell Agata of her plan. Perhaps Agata could come with them.

Agata was turning to go. Miranda caught her wrist. "Aunt Agata." Agata looked down at her, her nostrils flaring, but Miranda went on before she could speak. "Do you remember that day in the orchards outside of the city, when my mother fell? I dreamed of it, last night. I was only small, but I remember. She was beautiful, wasn't she?"

Agata's eyes grew wide and then narrowed. "She was beautiful. You look nothing like her." She shook her arm free of Miranda's grip. "Do not speak of her again."

The door slammed as she left. How long, Miranda despaired, would one have to dwell in another's mind to know them at all, to guess any part of what they felt?

Chapter 12

Miranda spent much of the rest of the day alone, until Dorothea scratched at the portal door.

"I have something I think will free your uncle from his prison," she said, poking her head out of the tunnels. "A powder they say can bring down walls, which the blacksmith helped me obtain in exchange for another few draughts of his stiff drink. We'll have to be careful with it, though, and leave as soon as he's out, in case anyone notices the noise." She looked down at Miranda. "Well? Are you coming?"

Miranda looked up at her, the edge of the tapestry she held forming a tent above them both. "I . . . isn't there anything I should bring? Anything we need?"

"You'll have gowns aplenty in Naples, and they won't do us any good while traveling. I've got clothes and caps for us, so we can move about looking like men. And some food, some supplies. That's all we'll need. It's all we can carry, anyway."

Miranda looked back at the room behind her. She had hated so much of her time here, but as she and Dorothea spent time within them, these rooms had begun to feel like home. "All right." She went to get the chair to climb up to the portal. "Wait—should I bring the veil?"

"Leave it." Dorothea moved back into the tunnels. "If we get to Naples, you'll never have to wear it again."

They clambered through the tunnels, noisy in their haste. The rain outside had begun to whip itself into a storm, and claps of thunder cracked beyond the castle walls. The furor of the tempest might disguise the clamor once Dorothea and Miranda used the powder, and it easily covered up the sound of their footsteps on the stone.

She cleared her throat. On all her previous visits to the tunnels, she had tried to be as silent as she could, but now she wanted to be heard. By one person, anyway. The person she had been longing for all her life, even when she knew it not.

"Mother?" Her voice sounded small in the engulfing darkness. "Mother, we've come to find you. We need your help."

No one replied. Dorothea took Miranda's hand as she summoned her courage to speak again. "Mother, please. Help us. We go to free Antonio. We're leaving the castle. If you can hear me—" She raised her voice. "If you can hear me, please show yourself. We need you now."

She tried anew around each curve in the path, to no avail. They came to the covered road, and she took up a torch from its entrance, casting the light about. They followed the twists and turns of the road until they came to what Miranda now recognized as Prospero's workrooms, only to find the iron door to the old laboratorium locked.

"It's never been locked before." She tried the handle, but it didn't budge. "Who locked it? Who came down here before us?"

"Who? Who?" The voice boomed down the halls, and thunder pealed in its wake. Lightning crackled through the high windows. "Do you remember the little white owl on the island, Miranda? The one you loved so well. He asked the same question, every morning, every evening." Miranda's hand fell, limp, from the door. "He asked and asked, and in the end the spirits silenced him. Too many questions, Miranda, bring ruin to us all."

Dorothea pressed her back against the door, her eyes following Prospero as he came down the passage, from the direction leading out of the castle, in the path of their escape. "Stay back," she said to Miranda in a low voice. "I'm going to use the pow—" She choked. "The p— The p—"

"What powder, little witch?" Prospero reached out his hand, twisting it, and the pouch at Dorothea's side snapped off its strap, sailing into his fingers. He crushed the pouch in his hand, crumbling it to dust. "With Moorish tricks and Sapphic temptations you did ensnare my only daughter, innocent as she was of the evils of this faithless world. Perhaps I am to blame, for I did not warn her of all the corruption that can twist the hearts of men."

He turned his eyes to Miranda, coming closer, step by careful step. "I did not tell you how blood can turn, go rancid and black, pitting brother against brother, and father against son. Your womanly mind is feeble, and fickle as the wind. You do not understand the bargain you've made, Miranda, but renounce it now, and I will forgive."

"She did not corrupt me." Miranda's voice shook, but she pressed on. "We saw what you did, Father. *I* saw. What became of my mother. How you violated her."

His laugh reverberated all around her. "False visions, crafted by your cunning companion." He came to stand before them, and Miranda clasped Dorothea's hand. "She thought I would not see, that her meager magic exceeded my own. Do you think anything happens in these walls without my knowing?" He snapped his fingers.

Miranda felt metal scrape beneath her wrist and pulled her hand back as if burned. There, from the door, a dozen iron hands reached out, grabbing hold of Dorothea, pinning her against the door.

"I command this castle. Every stone heeds my desires. Every beam and bolt bends to my will."

Dorothea yelled, but a gray hand slipped up to muffle the sound, clamping down upon her mouth. "She will tell you lies no longer, Miranda. Forget her tales, and listen to me. Mark my words. I will build a new world, and its capital will be this very castle. It will be Heaven brought to earth." He smiled. "This realm as it was meant to be. The paradise we lost, ere death entered this world."

"The dream," she gasped.

His smile grew. "The dream. Can't you see it, Miranda? A world more magical than the island, and greater by far."

Beside her, Dorothea struggled. Miranda stared into her father's face. "Death . . . undone."

"Yes."

"The way you undid my mother's death."

"Believe not whatever illusions you saw, Miranda." He moved his hand in a circle, and she saw the hands of iron tighten their grip. "I loved your mother well and gave her the greatest gift I could conceive. Who could fault a grieving husband for doing all he could for his virtuous wife? Who, after all, would not want more life?"

Miranda shook her head. "It was a half life." She reached out to slip her hand between the metal fingers on Dorothea's arm, to reassure her with a touch. "A life where she only existed for you, as a testament to your power, Prospero. Did you ever think how it would be for her? Did you ever think of what she wanted?"

"How dare you speak such foul words to your own father." He loomed above her, as he had loomed for all her life. "You will learn, Miranda. You will leave the witch, and you will learn your place."

"I will not."

He lifted both his hands, and she felt the fingers squirm. They dug into Dorothea's flesh, and Miranda clawed at them, losing her grip. "You're hurting her. Stop it!"

Prospero flexed his fingers slightly, and the digits closed around Dorothea's throat. "No! Let her go!"

Dorothea made a strangled noise. Miranda rushed toward her father, thrusting the torch into his face. It singed his beard, nearly catching flame. He knocked the torch from her grip and it tumbled to the stones, throwing his shadowed eyes and mocking mouth into relief as Miranda stared up at him.

"You will not forget this lesson, girl." He clenched his fists, and the fingers of iron contracted with them. "You have sleepwalked through this life and never known the suffering it brings, for I have protected you from its costs. But I will protect you no longer. You must learn, Miranda. You must listen—"

He hissed, dropping his hands, as sparks flew past them in the dark. Miranda spun to the right, to find the source of the light. She snatched up the torch and raised it high, but could see nothing.

She listened. She listened, and she heard it. The click-

ing, the clacking she had heard all those nights ago outside Antonio's cell, far off, growing ever closer.

Prospero squinted into the blackness before roaring
into its depths, flicking his wrists and sending a blast of
wind that whipped at Miranda's hair as it gusted down
the long passage.

"And so mine enemies send some rival magus, do
they? Begone! I have no time to play politics."

He raised his arms back to full height, and Miranda
spared a glance at Dorothea, whose hazel eyes bulged as
she tried futilely to break free of her restraints.

Tick. Tick. Tick. Miranda turned, throwing her torchlight once again into the dark. This time it limned the
form of the approaching figure, from the gleaming white
of its exposed feet to the iron mask it wore, its thin hands
outstretched, faint traces of golden light streaming from
between its fingers.

Prospero did not look towards the stranger, so focused
was he on his resuming his own speech. "You will learn,
girl. Attend me, and learn this lesson well. This castle, this
world, the very stuff of this universe, is mine to control,
and it is—"

"Not yours alone."

An arc of light flew straight at Dorothea. The hands
all around her retracted, melting back into the door, as
Prospero finally set his gaze upon the advancing figure.

Its voice was ragged, its speech half-slurred, but there was no mistaking it.

Beatrice, the once-dead duchess of Milan, had returned for her daughter at last.

Dorothea fell to the floor, gasping. Miranda ran to her side, pulling her up, away from the door, as Bice slammed it open. Miranda heard banging within the workrooms and knew what her mother had done. She had unlocked Antonio's door, as she must have unlocked the door to the laboratorium on Miranda's visits before. She had been with her all this time. Miranda had never been alone.

Prospero's sea-blue eyes were frozen on the figure's face. "Bice . . ." He recovered himself. "My beautiful wife. Returned from death, and waiting for me still. You have suffered, I know, while I have been away, without my magic to heal you, but now that I rule once more—"

"I learned to heal myself, Prospero." Her mother advanced, her sticklike limbs moving like spider legs. "My lesions and my rotting bits. This body that you left me with. Did you think you had gotten them all? Your books, your beloved texts? Did you not remember all those you had missed, hidden in your secret stores, down here in the depths?" She drew in a deep draught of air, as if the words had left her lungs weak. "I had so much time . . . to learn. Only . . . time. Endless . . . time."

"And we will have more." Prospero stretched his hands towards her. "Much more. Embrace me, fair Beatrice, and rule by my side as we bring magic to this profane plane."

She shook her head. "You are lost, Prospero. Your sins, both committed and as yet undone, number more than the stars." She lashed out, the light from her fingertips arcing, this time bringing Prospero to his knees. He fell heavily, and Miranda almost cried out, for still he was her father, and still she could remember the love she once felt for him, before all this, before she knew the truth of all that he had done. His great shaggy head rose, and he tried to lift his own hands, but Miranda's mother kept them pinned to the stone as she closed in. In the workrooms, Miranda heard a stirring. Antonio was moving within.

"So you've learned a few tricks." Prospero licked his lips. "But you are no match for me, Bice. After all, I taught you all you know." He began to hum, and from the stones around Beatrice's feet, talons of stone rose, ripping at her ankles with jagged claws. Miranda gasped, but her mother stepped free of them easily.

"You let your guard down, Prospero." She snapped her wrists, and twin streaks of light hit the ground, sending the stone hands back into the floor. "You believed your-self invincible. But you're weak now, aren't you? You used your power to speed your way back from Lyon, and to create this storm, for you could never resist such sound and fury." The long bones of her toes tapped against the rock. "You are old, and winded, and your body still obeys the natural laws, unlike mine. You could never overcome that, could you?" She raised her hands, rotating her wrists, and Prospero's eyes bulged.

"Set me free." Prospero's voice no longer rumbled, and Miranda saw his muscles strain under the force of her mother's magic. "Please, Bice—if you show me mercy, I will change. I will give up this magic, if that is your will. I swear it."

"Set you free, and again you will weave your lies. Again you will desecrate graves and subjugate daughters and escape your rightful sentencing by the skin of your silver tongue."

"I will not, I swear it." He looked towards Miranda, his eyes wild. "I sought to renounce my art, truly, before we returned to these shores. I can do it again. I will surrender it all, here and now, if you only let me go."

"No more." She rubbed her fingers together, and Miranda saw the bits of bone shining through. "Words are thy power and thy curse, Prospero. You speak too much and listen too little. Speak no more."

Prospero gaped like a fish. He kecked, but no sound came from his mouth. The lightning from the windows above sliced across his face, and Miranda saw the veins beneath his pale skin, the blood pooling in his eyes.

She kept her arms tight around Dorothea as she heard Antonio's dragging footsteps emerging from the cell. Bice slipped a hand into her strange, funereal garment and pulled out a shining blade, handing it to Antonio, who accepted it, his eyes never leaving Bice's mask.

Beatrice crossed to where Miranda and Dorothea crouched and extended a skeletal hand. Miranda took it, shivering, and her mother led them both away from where Antonio stood over Prospero, back down the passage to the castle. "Come away, Miranda, and rest now. Let men settle the affairs of men."

They slipped into the darkness, and the sound of Prospero's screams did not follow them.

Epilogue

"It's a beautiful palace."

Dorothea and Miranda stood together on the loggia that overlooked the sea. Miranda nodded, relishing the feel of the breeze on her bare skin. "It is."

"And Ferdinand seems kind."

Miranda swallowed. "He is." She had been glad to see Ferdinand again; glad for a friend, for someone who welcomed the sight of her face, after all these weeks of living in shadow. He had been overjoyed to see her, and to greet her lady-in-waiting, and her "aunt," whose body, Miranda explained to him in a whisper, had been badly disfigured by an accident in her youth, and who was now ashamed to go anywhere without every inch of it covered.

Antonio had not accompanied them to Naples, though he had sent them with a powerful contingent of gifted guards. He stayed behind to tend to the turmoil in Milan, the uproar caused by the mysterious murder of the old duke. Miranda had asked if there would be rebellion, if Milan's subjects would object to his reclamation of the dukedom, and he had shaken his head. "Chaos will reign, for a time. But then, that is Italy. Milan will endure."

All Antonio's lieutenants had been waiting by, waiting for their chance to push out Prospero's scanty forces within the ranks of Milan, and so the transition had already begun. Miranda left the city satisfied that its future was ensured, that her choice had been the right one. But in the night, she still dreamed of paradise. In the darkness, she still heard an old voice calling, and she awoke, more mornings than not, with tears in her eyes.

Dorothea knew this. They had let Dorothea stay in Miranda's room, in a supposedly separate bed, when Miranda explained how the death of her father had wracked her nerves. She and Dorothea had not spoken of what might come next, now that they were safe in Naples. After almost losing Dorothea again, at the hands of her own father, Miranda was loath to destroy their fragile bit of peace. Part of her longed for this life, watching the sun set over the sea from her fine palace, Dorothea by her side and all the power of the Neapolitan crown at hand. But the ocean breeze made her restless, raised in her again the desire to run, to swim, to dive into the blue waters wearing nothing but her skin, an act that Ferdinand would surely never condone. She might teach him the pleasures of discarding courtly life, of casting off titles and cumbersome jewels and embracing the gifts of the sun and the earth and the stars every once in a while. Yet she felt she would soon tire of such teaching, of instructing someone in truths that ought to be evident, of guiding through ignorance a person who should be better equipped to navigate the nuances of the world.

As, perhaps, Dorothea had tired of teaching her.

~

Miranda's mother stayed in the room next to where Miranda and Dorothea slept, and Miranda had spent their first night talking with her until the early hours of the morning, learning all that had occurred in the dozen years they had been apart.

"I never surrendered hope that you would return to me," Bice said, her voice hushed, which was the tone that seemed to pain her least. She had taken off the mask, at Miranda's request. Her eyes were glazed with a whitish-blue film, and her skin speckled with spots of decay, but she was still Miranda's mother. Still her spirit endured, though Miranda wished she could help her find a better life than this one lived in the shadows. "If the dead can rise, I knew you could come back to me. So I waited. I read. I prepared, for I knew Prospero would be preparing, too. Remember: I knew better than anyone what he could do. I knew no sea and storm could stop him."

"And you visited Antonio. You told him not to tell me."

Beatrice nodded. "I did. I feared . . . I feared you would not understand. That even if I found a way to stop your father, you would never come with me, never escape him. You had to learn the truth yourself. And I did not want you to see me this way." She looked down. "It's why I brought you to the gallery, that night at the ball. Perhaps it was foolish, but I wanted you to remember me as I seem to be in that frame. Living. Beautiful. Not—" She gestured to her face. "Like this."

Miranda took her hand, ignoring the involuntary frisson of repulsion she felt every time she touched the clammy flesh of her mother's palm, which reminded her of the skin of that little frog from so very long ago. "All I care about is that we're back together again. I only wish Agata—"

Beatrice shook her head. "Agata has suffered enough. Knowing I still walk this earth would only bring her sorrow. I pray she will find peace." She cleared her throat, as she often did, for too many words seemed to strain it. "Let us talk . . . of happier things. Your wedding plans. Are the preparations for the ball near done?"

"They are." The wedding ball was to be held in two days' time, and Miranda had been caught in a whirlwind of ribbons and silk as the ladies around her rushed to fit her for her gown and attend to other plans. Only her nights were her own, and she was grateful to spend them with her mother and Dorothea.

Bice tilted her head, her vitreous eyes fixed on Miranda's face. "You don't seem happy."

"I am." The words rang hollow. Miranda tried again. "I am. Happy that this sad tale is come to an end. Milan is saved. Naples will be joined with Milan, and all of Italy will be stronger for it."

"You speak of politics, Miranda. The chessboard of kings and queens, where all of us are only pieces." Her mother reached out to tilt Miranda's chin up. "What about you? Are you happy?"

"I . . . I don't know. What is it, to be happy? I hardly know my own mind, after so many years alone, with only my father as a guide, and he so often plunged me into darkness. Who knows what I do out of fear, and what out of love? Half my life is lost, my history submerged."

"But you do love." Bice's eyes searched her face. "You know Ferdinand loves you."

Miranda sighed. "He tells me so, every day. He wrote it in his letters. I read every one. But he was writing to a painting, Mother. He may as well be in love with a portrait hanging in the galleries. Nothing he says penetrates beyond that. He talks of the beauty of the children I will bear, of the favorable alliance our marriage will make." She looked down at their joined hands. "He has cast me in the role of queen, and my lines are already written."

"And it isn't the role you want."

"I don't think so."

"You aren't sure that you love him."

"No."

"For your heart belongs to another."

Miranda startled, raising her head. Bice laughed, a rattling sound that came from deep in her throat. "My heart may not beat, Miranda, but I can still tell what love looks like. You love her, and I understand why."

"But—in this world—"

"Love is life, Miranda." Her mother blinked, the motion slow and strange to see. "It matters not in what form it comes."

~

Dorothea had been quiet since they had come to Naples. In their room the past two nights she had lain beside Miranda but had made no move to embrace her, to kiss and caress the way she had in Milan. Perhaps, Miranda feared, their brief romance was at its end. Looking at Dorothea's face, bathed in the early-evening glow as they stood on the loggia gazing out at the horizon, she wanted nothing more than to reach out, to stroke Dorothea's cheek and ask her to stay.

And yet she couldn't ask Dorothea to remain in a gilded cage. She couldn't ask her to risk her skin by staying too close to Miranda's side, by hiding who she was, day after day, night after night. Already Miranda had overhead murmured questions in Ferdinand's court about which of Milan's noble families Dorothea hailed from and knew they could not keep up the ruse for long.

"Dorothea."

"Hmm?" Dorothea was still looking out to sea, over the cerulean waters of the bay. In the distance loomed the green mass of Vesuvius, which Ferdinand had told Miranda was a volcano. He'd promised to take Miranda to see the old Roman towns its ash had covered, and she could picture it in her mind's eye: a rare outing from her pretty palace, encircled by its palm trees and terraced rows of oleander and jasmine and violets. License to walk free for an afternoon, maybe even to dirty the hem of her fine cloak as she bent to examine one of the bodies Ferdinand said he was sure would make her faint. That was adventure, for a princess. That was her life as a future queen.

"I was thinking." Her mouth felt parched by the salty air. "Now that we're here—now that I'm to be queen—I could help you go anywhere you want. Do whatever you want to do. Ferdinand says we have ships, lots of them, and plenty of gold to spend. If there was somewhere you wanted to go, I could help you get there. I couldn't in Milan, but—I can help you here."

Dorothea had turned during Miranda's stumbling speech, watching her with an impassive gaze. "You're sending me away?"

"No, I—" Miranda reached out but then pulled back her hand, suddenly afraid of anyone—a servant, a noble, Ferdinand himself—interrupting this stolen moment. "I'm asking you. Where you want to go. You can't—it's not fair, me asking you to stay here. You know it isn't. I want you to, I do—"

"But you can't."

Miranda's voice was little more than a whisper. "I can't."

Dorothea looked at her a long time. She could see every freckle on Dorothea's nose, every line in her lips, those lips she had kissed only a few nights before. The edges of Dorothea's features began to blur, softening and shading like the lines of a painting, and it was only then Miranda realized that she was beginning to cry.

Beneath them the waves beat on. Dorothea turned back to them, away from Miranda, and Miranda could hardly hear her as she began to speak. "I never told you how my mother died, did I?"

Miranda took a step forward, up to the railing, wiping away a tear. "No. You never did."

Dorothea's eyes stayed on the sea. "She drowned. We

were living in a city a lot like this. A place called Smyrna. A beautiful city on the ocean, where she loved to swim every day. But one morning her body washed up on the shore. Mariam wouldn't let me see it. The people in our neighborhood all said she drowned herself, but my brother, Beni, said she went out with a man, a stranger, earlier that night, and he was certain she'd been murdered."

Miranda's breath caught in her throat. "Do you think she was?"

"I don't know. She was tired, by the end. Tired of searching for a place to call her own." Dorothea's voice was weary, and Miranda wondered how well she'd been sleeping these past two nights, if she had remained wakeful and restless while Miranda slumbered on. "My mother didn't want to settle down, and she refused to marry. It's why we never stayed still. Well, that and other trouble along the road. She dreamed of seeing the world. But all she saw is lost. Her pages, burned. Her memories, drowned in the Aegean Sea. Maybe Mariam carries her poetry on, to the new continent, or Beni tells her tales around campfires. But I'll never know what they sow. We're scattered to the wind, like seeds in a storm."

"I could help you follow them." Miranda did reach out now, curling her pinkie finger around Dorothea's. "Anywhere you wanted to go, Dorothea. I could get you there."

"I appreciate the offer, my queen," said Dorothea. Her voice held only the faintest lilting mockery. "But living in a French war camp hardly seems the life for me, and the stories they bring from the Americas hold horrors greater than here."

"Surely there must be someplace, though. Somewhere you'd like to go. Somewhere better."

Dorothea shook her head. "I've been so many places, and it's always masks. Masks and masks, until you lose your true face. I want it back, Miranda. My face. I want to live as I am, somewhere in this world. And I don't know where to go. I don't know anywhere I could be free."

The sun was slipping from them now, lost in the darkening waters roiling far below their feet. Somewhere out there lay the only real home Miranda had ever known. Somewhere in the night, Caliban roasted fish over a fire, and the spirits joined their voices in chorus, singing silver-sweet melodies. She could almost hear them, those euphonious lullabies that had carried her to sleep. They echoed through her mind, along with Antonio's last words to her, the words that had been ringing in her head ever since their escape from Milan.

He had embraced her at last, just before they left for Naples. They had kept their departure a secret, to conceal Bice, to protect Miranda, and only Antonio bade them farewell. His arms were stiff around her back, but he leaned in close, whispering one last request in her ear. "Promise me. If you return to the island—if you find his bones—bury him. Let him rest." He pulled back, searching her face with dark, haunted eyes. "Please. Let him rest."

In all these long weeks in Italy, in all the time since they had left, she had never considered returning to the island. It lived on no map. She could not trace a route back to its shores. But she knew its birds, she realized. Birds that nested nowhere else, flocks that could lead her back, if she got close enough. And she had two magicians by her side, who together surely could find an enchanted isle.

She had thought it her duty to stay. To become queen, and rule justly, and carry on the aims of that noble civilization of which her father had so often spoken. But the island had civilization, too. It had Caliban, who she still missed, and with whom she wished to make amends. It had Ariel, who perhaps she could one day count as a friend, or at the very least an ally. It was thick with colonies of frogs, and clouds of bats, and thriving swarms of bees and butterflies and gnats. Miranda had not realized that she even missed the gnats. And if Dorothea came with her—if her mother did, too—she would have a family. Maybe, if they all went together, if Miranda could somehow convince Dorothea to leave the mainland behind, it would be enough. Maybe she didn't need anything more, for in the whole world she could not think of what she'd want, besides the sea, and the sky, and her mother safe, and Dorothea by her side, somewhere they could live their own lives.

"There may be . . . one place. A place we could go. Together."

Dorothea looked up. "And where would that be?"

"The island."

"Caliban's island."

"Yes."

"The enchanted island, in the middle of the treacherous sea."

"Yes."

Dorothea stared at her and then burst out laughing. "I knew there was a reason I loved you. You're even madder than me."

Miranda felt a grin spread across her face, and she clutched Dorothea's hand tight. "I mean it. We could live as we like, and no one would ever find us."

"Start anew? Make a better world?"

"Yes!"

"And if Caliban refuses? If he wishes to keep his island his own?"

"If he refuses us—" If he turned them away, she would not try to trick him or cajole him into letting them stay.

She hadn't begun to pay for the sins of her father, and she would not compound them by forcing her way onto Caliban's land. "If he refuses, we'll venture on. We'll find someplace. Some corner of the world no one else wants." She could see it in her mind. A distant jetty beneath gray skies. A thatched cottage on a rocky coast, with smoke rising from the rustic chimney. Three women at the end of everything, holding fast to the edge of the earth, in thunder, lightning, and in rain.

"It might work." Dorothea pressed her fingertips into Miranda's palm. "If your mother helps us. If her magic is strong. But first, Miranda, you must make me a promise."

"What is it?"

"If Caliban lets us ashore—if he accepts us into his home—you must learn his language. You must listen, rather than speak. Unlearn the lines of your father. Watch Caliban write his own in the sand. Learn his language, and mine, and maybe we can create this new land you dream of."

"But—" Miranda floundered. "Caliban has no language. We—I mean, my father—taught him everything he knows. The name of the sun and moon, and the stars. He knew nothing of these, before we came."

"Do you believe his mother knew no poetry? That she never whispered or sang him to sleep? Ask him, Miranda. His mother wrote, or spoke her truths to him. Language isn't bound in books. It's in hands and tongues and looks just as surely as in holy scripts. Caliban has a language. It's you who ignore its import, his greater meaning."

The skin on the back of Miranda's neck prickled. She wanted to deny Dorothea's words, to tell her that she was wrong, that Miranda could never have missed so much, all those years living with Caliban in their island home. And yet there were places on the island she had never gone, places where the spirits hissed a name like *Sycorax* and flies hung thick around the mouths of sunken, swampy caves. There were symbols carved into gnarled trees in the deep woods, and she'd never known if her father or the witch or Caliban himself had put them there. She had stopped asking long ago, in the face of her father's rage. Now she could give voice to all she'd wondered. Now, for the first time, she and Caliban could speak freely, without fear, without restriction.

"I promise." She threaded her fingers through Dorothea's as the sky above them turned from blue to black. "Wherever we go. I'll learn to speak his language, and yours."

~

The two young men were escorting a leper to a nearby lazaretto and were in need of a boat. The dockmaster in the port of Valletta sold them the first decent vessel he found on hand, to clear them from the harbor as quickly as he could. It was an old rowboat, and they paid him far too much for it, but perhaps it would get them where they were going. They didn't seem to know how far that was, or much about sailing at all. He watched them head out to the horizon, their unlucky cargo covered in a shroud, and then turned his attention to other things, to the bustle of boatswains and passengers.

As soon as they were far enough from the shore, Duriya let the glamour drop. She had been happier than Miranda had ever seen her, ever since they had made their escape from Naples, to Palermo, and then to Malta. The sprezzatura in her step delighted Miranda, as did the fact that she had at last asked Miranda to call her Duriya. She taught Miranda to say it properly, only laughing a little as Miranda tried, again and again, until she finally got it right, and Duriya rewarded her with a kiss.

Beatrice had come willingly, though she only smiled when Miranda explained that the enchanted island might have properties that could help her heal, could help her live some fuller kind of life. "Perhaps" was all she said. She seemed to enjoy the journey, and as they made their way farther out to sea, she kept the waters calm. Beneath her mask Miranda could see that her eyes were closed, and on occasion she gave directions, bringing them closer and closer to the power she could feel emanating from the isle.

They rowed for two hours, maybe more, until a movement in the sky caught Miranda's eye. She looked up and saw a flock of birds passing overhead, wheeling about on their expansive patterned wings. Their feathers were purplish-blue, of a hue she had seen nowhere on the mainland. They cried to one another, and she recognized the sound. These were the birds she knew. She heard their songs still in her dreams.

"There." Miranda took Duriya's hand and pointed to the winged beings. "Let's follow them home."

So the monster, her mother, and her lover took hold of the oars and rowed their way to shore.

About the Author

Laura Lamb

KATHARINE DUCKETT's fiction has appeared in *Uncanny, Apex Magazine, Interzone, PseudoPod,* and various anthologies. She is also the guest fiction editor for the Disabled People Destroy Fantasy issue of *Uncanny*. She hails from East Tennessee, has lived in Turkey and Kazakhstan, and attended Hampshire College in Amherst, Massachusetts, where she majored in minotaurs. *Miranda in Milan* is her first book. She currently resides in Brooklyn with her wife.

TOR·COM

Science fiction. Fantasy. The universe. And related subjects.

*

More than just a publisher's website, *Tor.com* is a venue for **original fiction, comics,** and **discussion** of the entire field of SF and fantasy, in all media and from all sources. Visit our site today—and join the conversation yourself.